# Everybody Kills Somebody Sometime

# Everybody Kills Somebody Sometime

## ROBERT J. RANDISI

Thomas Dunne Books
St. Martin's Minotaur   New York

THOMAS DUNNE BOOKS.
An imprint of St. Martin's Press.

EVERYBODY KILLS SOMEBODY SOMETIME. Copyright © 2006 by Robert J. Randisi. All rights reserved. Printed in the United States of America. No part of this book may be used or reproduced in any manner whatsoever without written permission except in the case of brief quotations embodied in critical articles or reviews. For information, address St. Martin's Press, 175 Fifth Avenue, New York, N.Y. 10010.

www.thomasdunnebooks.com
www.minotaurbooks.com

Design by Phil Mazzone

ISBN-13: 978-0-312-33862-6
ISBN-10: 0-312-33862-7

First Edition: November 2006

10  9  8  7  6  5  4  3  2  1

*To Dean, Frank and Sammy*
*Thanks for the memories, pallies*

Everybody
Kills Somebody
Sometime

# Prologue

WHEN THE BUILDING IMPLODED it was like they ripped my fuckin' heart out.

I watched as forty-four years of history—forty-three of which I was a part—collapsed in a heap of mortar-and-brick rubble. But I was surprised when my shoulders came down with the building, and my insides unclenched.

Only a few hours ago I was standing at my post in the pit among the blackjack tables. Forty-three years ago Jack Entratter had hired me, and three hours ago the current owner, Sheldon Adelson, had been decent enough to walk out ahead of me and allow me to be the last person to leave.

At seventy-six I didn't have that much time left to make memories, but that was one I wanted to have. Now I stood under the great Sands marquee with the other employees who had hung around—Sheldon standing on my right, Las Vegas great Wayne Newton on my left—to watch as the walls came tumbling down.

Suddenly the air was filled with dirt and dust. People began to scatter pretty quickly, some coughing and covering their mouths.

"Come on, Eddie," Sheldon said, grabbing my arm. "Let's get away from here. This stuff's not gonna be good for your asthma."

I started coughing as Sheldon dragged me away and suddenly I felt my legs going out from under me. From my other side I felt Wayne Newton's strong hands take hold of me and the two practically carried me away from the scene.

"Eddie?" I heard Sheldon call.

All of a sudden I wasn't sure where I was. I turned my head and instead of seeing a pile of rubble I saw the great Sands Hotel as it had stood thirty-six years ago, in it's glorious heyday, when Frank and Dino and Sammy were there, when I was a helluva lot younger and stronger and times were better and exciting. . . .

"Eddie?" I heard Sheldon say. "Come back."

But fuck it, I didn't want to. . . .

# One

WHEN I SPOTTED JOEY BISHOP walking toward me across the Sands casino floor, I figured he wasn't heading for a blackjack table. Although a member of Sinatra's Rat Pack—he called himself a "mascot" while Sinatra called him "The Hub of the Wheel"—Joey didn't drink or gamble, and he didn't party much. Even after the shows in the Copa Room—which Sinatra had started calling "The Summit"—while the others went out and partied the night away, Joey usually went back to his room. I'd heard him refer to himself more than once as a "Go-Home" guy.

So, to see him walking toward the blackjack tables meant one of two things: either he had a friend playing, or he was coming to see me.

I'm Eddie Gianelli. In Brooklyn they used to call me Eddie G, and I guess it was only natural the moniker would follow me to Vegas. For years I had come to Las Vegas like everybody else, to see some shows and play a little blackjack, but eventually I learned that it was Vegas itself I loved. It was the smell and the feel, the limitless food and sex and opportunities, the *pulse* of the place, not just the action, so twelve years ago I came and stayed. I got some jobs in casinos, working my way up to blackjack dealer in places like the Flamingo, the Desert Inn and the Sahara, but when the Sands opened its doors in 1952, I hustled my ass to put in my application for a job.

The call did not come for a year, but once I got in I used five of the last seven years to work myself up to pit boss, where I am now—and pretty damned happy about it, too.

When Joey reached the tables he waved at me. We met over a covered table that had not yet been opened. It was still early in the evening, and all of the tables weren't in use yet. The slot machines, lining the walls all around us, were likewise only about half in use, with only the occasional sound of coins hitting the tray or bells going off. The slot machines were traditionally played by women—wives, girlfriends, both—who were trying to win a few bucks while their men dropped real money at the tables. Some Vegas insiders were predicting bigger things for the slots in the future, but I had my doubts about that. To me, the real money was always going to be at the table.

As usual, Joey was decked out in a suit that would have cost me a week's salary, maybe more.

"Eddie G, my buddy," Joey said, extending his hand.

"Buddy" was stretching a point. I knew Joey, of course—knew who he was, and who he hung around with, and had seen him in the casino, though never gambling. We'd had conversations and coffee together once or twice. I knew Joey like I knew a lot of people because a total of twelve years working on the strip had put me in the know.

"Joey," I said. "What can I do for you, pal?" What the hell? If he could lay it on thick with "buddy" I could do the same with "pal."

"Well, it's not exactly what you can do for me, Eddie, but for a friend of mine."

"A friend?" I knew who Joey's friends were. "Uh, just who are we talkin' about here, Joey?"

He shrugged. "I'm talkin' about Frank."

"I don't understand," I said. "What the hell would Frank Sinatra want with me?"

"Well . . . can we go someplace for a cup of coffee?" Joey asked.

I checked my watch.

"I can meet you in the coffee shop in about twenty minutes. Can Mr. Sinatra wait that long?"

"Hey," Joey said, with another shrug, "if he has to wait, he has to wait. I'll see you in half an hour."

I knew that Joey Bishop was probably one of two people in Las Vegas who wasn't afraid of Frank Sinatra and his perceived connections to organized crime.

I also knew that I wasn't the second person.

I found Joey sitting alone in a booth in the back of the coffee shop. I was willing to bet that he had signed more than a few autographs while sitting there, but at the moment he was alone.

"Joey," I said, sitting opposite him.

"Thanks for coming."

The pretty waitress came over and I said, "Just coffee, Bev."

"Comin' up, Eddie."

Joey and I watched her walk away, firm ass twitching with every step. When it came right down to it, all the waitresses in the Sands were knockouts. It was something the owner, Jack Entratter, made damn sure of. Jack was a confirmed tits-and-ass man and, since I shared the same appreciation for a great set of knockers and a firm, round butt, it made working there even better, especially since most of them were single and available—and some of the married ones were, too.

As we watched Beverly walk away, the look on Joey's face never changed. He looked perpetually bored with life, even when he was performing. He was looking at her appreciatively, but one of the other things I knew about Joey Bishop was that he didn't cheat. It made him an even odder member of the Rat Pack, since those guys attracted babes like nobody's business.

"Okay, Joey," I said, "you've got my attention and nobody else can hear us. What's up?"

"Frank wants to talk to you."

"To me? Yeah, sure. What's the gag?"

"No gag, kiddo."

"What's it about?"

"That'll be between you and him."

"When?"

"Now." Joey looked at his watch. "He's in the steam room."

"The steam room?"

Sinatra had had the steam room built especially for him and his pals so they'd have something to do between shooting their new movie, *Ocean's 11*, and their Summit show in the Copa Room. Very few people beyond those five—Frank, Dino, Sammy, Peter Lawford and Joey—were ever allowed in there.

"Yep. We can go there right now, if you want." Joey made as if to rise.

"Hold your horses, Joe." I put my hand out to stop him.

"What? You wanna finish your coffee?"

"No," I said, "I'm just not sure I wanna go and meet Frank Sinatra."

Joey got comfortable again.

"Why not?"

"I don't know . . . what could he possibly want with me?" I asked.

"Eddie," he said, leaning forward, "you're not lettin' all those stories get to you, are you?"

"What stories?"

"You know," Joey said, touching his nose, "the Mafia, Giancana, all that stuff?"

The rumors about Frank Sinatra's connection to the mob had been around for years, even before they were supposed to have gotten him the part in *From Here to Eternity* that won him the Oscar and revived his career. There were many stories about that, but the one I'd heard the most was that Johnny Roselli had gone to studio head Harry Cohn's office and simply said, "Frank gets this part or we'll have you killed."

Did I believe it?

"No . . . well, maybe . . . I'm not all that sure . . . Joey, I just don't see what Frank—Mr. Sinatra—would want with me."

"I can't tell you that, Ed," Joey said. "Only Frank can."

"Well . . . I think I'm gonna have to pass, Joe," I said. "I mean . . . if that's all right?"

"Sure, it's all right," Joey said, with another characteristic shrug. "You don't wanna see him, don't see him. It's no skin off my nose."

"Okay," I said, "okay."

Bev came with my coffee and put it down, then walked away. Neither Joey nor I watched her, this time.

I dug into my pocket. "Lemme get the java—"

"Hey, I got it," Joey said, waving his hand. "Don't worry about it."

"I gotta get back to work."

"Sure," Joey said, "go."

I stood up, but didn't leave.

"You'll tell him I was, uh, flattered, but . . . I'm kinda busy—"

"Hey, Eddie," Joey said, spreading his hands, "forget about it, okay?"

"Okay . . . then I'll go back to work."

"Sure."

I started to walk away, then turned to look back at him. He was still sitting in the booth. He smiled and waved.

# *Two*

I WAS ONLY BACK at my pit half an hour when one of the other pit bosses, Richie Castellani, came over and whispered in my ear, "Boss wants you, G. Now."

The boss was Jack Entratter, who had left his job as assistant manager and bouncer at the Copacabana in New York to come to Vegas to run the Sands Hotel and Casino for Frank Costello—or so the story goes. All of the entertainers who went through the Copa while Jack was there had come to love him, so not only had Frank, Dean, Sammy and the others made the Sands their place in Las Vegas but others, too, like Lena Horne, Nat King Cole, Milton Berle, Danny Thomas, Tony Bennett and Dean's old partner, Jerry Lewis.

Richie stepped into the pit and I left and headed for Jack's office. I knew what this was about. Entratter and Sinatra were friends, and Frank was a two-percent owner in the casino; I had the feeling Joey Bishop had gone over my head.

I knocked on Entratter's door and he shouted, "Come in!"

If Entratter was really running the Sands for Costello, he was the perfect choice. He wasn't Italian, and nobody would ever take him for one. Jack was six three or four, a hulking brute of a man who had been left bandy-legged by the childhood disease osteomyelitis. As a twenty-six year old in 1940 he had signed on as bouncer at the Copa and over the next twelve years had moved up to assistant manager without giving up his bouncer job. At thirty-eight he had left the Copa to take over the newest casino in Vegas, the Sands. Now Jack was forty-six and ruled the Sands with an iron hand, but he was even better known as a showman. There were times he even got up on stage with the Pack. I envied him that. I was a shower singer who dreamed about being on stage.

He was sitting behind his desk, alone in the office, when I entered. His suit was sharp, but it lost some of its edges because it was on Entratter's body. His tie was askew and his shoulders were threatening his seams.

"What the hell are you tryin' to do to me?" he demanded.

"Boss?"

"Who's my best friend in the world?"

Well, the answer to that varied from week to week, but I knew what he wanted to hear.

"Frank Sinatra."

"You bet your ass, Frank Sinatra," he growled. "So when my best friend in the world asks you for help, what do you tell him? You tell him no."

"Well, uh, I told Joey I'd like to take a pass," I tried to explain. "I never did talk to Mr. Sinatra—"

"Don't you think you should?" Entratter asked. "I mean, before you take a pass shouldn't you find out what you're takin' a pass from?" He made it sound like the most reasonable request in the world.

"Jack, I—"

"You work for me, don't ya, Eddie?"

"Well, yeah, Jack, I do, but—"

"So if I ordered you to talk to Frank you would, right?"

"I, uh, well, sure—"

"But I ain't gonna do that."

"You're not?"

"Siddown, Eddie."

I sat across from him.

"You're from New York, right?" He knew that, but I answered the question, anyway.

"That's right. Brooklyn."

"I never saw you at the Copa."

"I never went," I said. "It was more than I could afford back then."

"Yeah, it was kinda expensive."

For a moment Entratter retreated a dozen or so years inside his head, then shook off the reverie and looked at me again. "I ain't gonna order you to talk to Frank, kid." He called me "kid" a lot, even though he was only about six years older than I was.

"I appreciate that, Jack—"

"I'm gonna ask ya to do it as a favor to me, Eddie," he went on, cutting me off. "Go and talk to him, see what he wants. If you can help him, help him. If not . . ." he shrugged.

I owed Entratter a lot and he knew it. That's why he was asking me instead of telling me.

"You're the man here in Vegas," Jack said, then. "You know everybody there is to know in this town. You got it wired. Hookers, pimps, valets, doormen, high rollers and bums, you know 'em all. If anybody can help Frank it's Eddie G—"

"Okay, Jack, okay," I said. "Geez, enough. A guy can only take so much stroking. I get the picture. I'm your man."

"Great!' Jack said, clapping his big hands together. "Joey's down in the casino waitin' for you."

"You knew I'd say yes?"

"If ya hadn't," Jack said, "I woulda ordered ya to. But I knew I could count on you, kid. Now get out. I got work to do."

I headed for the door, but never made it.

"Eddie."

"Yeah, Boss." I turned to face him with my back to the door.

"I'm curious," he said. "Why'd you refuse in the first place?"

"Like I said," I replied, "I'm from Brooklyn."

"So?"

"Frank's from Jersey." I made a face.

"Get out!"

I left Jack's office and made my way back to the casino floor. Joey was seated at an empty blackjack table, waiting for me. As I approached him he stood up, his face expressionless.

"Steam room?" I asked.

"Steam room," he said.

# Three

THE STEAM ROOM was in the bowels of the Sands. Since it was so exclusive—just the Rat Pack and their close friends—I half expected there to be a guard on duty. According to Jack Entratter I was "the man," but I'd never been down there before.

When we got there I spotted some robes hanging on the wall. On the backs were written the names "Smokey," "The Needler," "The Dago" and "Charlie the Seal." There was an empty peg, which I assumed would hold Frank's robe, but hanging on it at the moment was a shoulder holster.

"Charlie the Seal?' I asked.

"That's Peter," Joey explained. "He has a smoker's cough."

"The Needler has to be you."

"Correct."

"The Dago is Dean; Smokey is Sammy?"

"Right," Joey said, "because Sammy smokes."

"Right. And what does Frank have on the back of his robe?"

"What else? 'The Leader.' "

"And who gave out the names?"

"Frank."

"Figures."

Joey walked to the robes on the wall and took down "The Dago."

"This looks like your size."

"I—I can't wear Dean Martin's robe," I said.

"Wrong," Joey said. "You can't wear mine or Sammy's because they'd be too short."

"But—Dean Martin?" Joey didn't know it—few people did—but I was a huge Dean Martin fan. In my opinion his level of cool was head-and-shoulders above the rest of the Rat Pack combined.

"Okay," Joey said, with a shrug, "wear Peter's."

He started to put "The Dago" back on the wall and I said, "No wait . . . I'll wear Dean's."

Joey smiled and handed me the robe.

"I'll be upstairs," he said. "Frank wants to talk to you alone. Think you can find your way back out?"

"I'm sure I can."

"Then I'll see you upstairs."

As Joey left I undressed, put on Dean Martin's robe and then approached the steam room door. I wasn't sure what to do at that point, knock or just walk in. I hesitated, almost knocked, then figured, "What the hell," and walked right in.


"Over here."

In just two words the familiar voice made chills run up my spine. The Jersey accent was never very far removed. Being from New York I recognized even a hint of it. I'd been out of Brooklyn for twelve years and still hadn't completely lost my accent.

The steam was kind of thick but I followed his voice and gradually he came into view.

The Leader.

The Chairman of the Board.

Sinatra.

Frank.

"Eddie Gianelli?"

"That's right."

Frank extended his hand. For a moment I wondered if I was supposed to kiss it, but in the end I just shook his hand. I was surprised at how small it felt in mine. I was also surprised at how frail he looked, sitting there in his robe.

"How's your bird?" This was Rat Pack-ese for "How are ya?" They were so cool they had their own language.

"Good, Frank. I'm good."

"Have a seat."

Rather than join him on the set of risers he was sitting on I climbed the ones adjacent to him. He was seated on the upper most level of his, so I chose to sit one from the top on my side. Later I realized it had been a kind of unwitting deference.

"First, thanks for coming."

"No problem." I was already sweating, probably from the steam.

"Here," he said, tossing me a towel. "It's clean."

"Thanks." I caught it and wiped my face. Okay, so maybe I was nervous.

"I see Joey gave you Dean's robe."

"Yeah," I said, "I hope that's okay. It's the only one that fit."

"Hey, it's jake with me," Frank said, "and I'm sure Dino won't mind."

I was kind of annoyed at my reaction to meeting him, being in the same room with him—the steam room. I was impressed, there was no denying it, but I'd once heard him refer to himself as just "a lounge singer." That's what he was, an entertainer. I mean, it wasn't as if I was in the presence of Ike, or even Joe DiMaggio, for Chrissake.

But then again, he wasn't just some entertainer, he was Frank Sinatra. By anyone's standards, that was big. By Las Vegas standards, it was huge!

"I guess you're wonderin' why I asked you down here," Frank said.

"Yeah, you could say I'm curious."

He laughed. "Yeah, I guess you would be."

Sinatra paused long enough to wipe his forehead on the towel he was wearing around his thin shoulders. His chest looked almost concave to me. I wondered if being on the big movie screen added weight, or bulk, or if it was just a matter of the image being so big.

"They call you Eddie G, right?"

"That's right."

"Eddie, I'm told you know a lot of people in Las Vegas."

"I suppose that's true."

"And I'm told you can get things done."

"Well . . . you can get things done, Mr. Sinatra—"

"Oh no, Eddie," Sinatra said, waving his forefinger at me, "no, no, no . . ." He pursed his lips, the way I'd seen him do in countless movies. "Not 'Mr. Sinatra.' Call me Frank."

"Okay . . . Frank."

"You're from New York, aren't ya?"

"Yes, Mr.—yeah, Frank, I'm from New York—Brooklyn, to be exact."

"I didn't catch the accent the first time we talked, but I got it now."

"I've been away a while," I said. "It comes and goes."

"You don't mind that I call you Eddie, do ya?"

"No," I said. "I don't mind."

"Okay, Eddie," Frank said, "I need a favor."

"Name it."

Frank frowned.

" 'Name it,' means you'll do it, no matter what I say. Did Jack tell you that you had to do what I asked?"

"As a matter of fact," I answered, "what he said was he'd consider it a favor if I came and listened to what you had to say."

"So you had a choice."

"Yeah," I said, "I could come and listen, or eat shit for a while before he forgave me."

"Would he fire you?"

"Nah, he wouldn't fire me," I said, "I'm too good at my job, but he'd make me miserable for a while."

"But he didn't say that, exactly?"

"It was understood."

"Well, understand this," Frank said. "I'm gonna ask you a favor, and you've got a choice. You can say yes, or you can say no. No consequences. Understand?"

"Yes, sir—Frank."

"So nothing's 'understood,' " Frank said. "Everything's clear?"

I hesitated a moment, getting it straight in my head, then said, "Everything is clear."

"Okay." He wiped his forehead again, then leaned forward.

# *Four*

"WHAT'S THE FAVOR, Frank?" My curiosity was killing me, but I tried to appear cool. It wasn't easy, though, since I was in a steam room with Mr. Cool, himself.

"A friend of mine has been receiving death threats," Frank explained. "I want you to find out who's sendin' them."

"You need a private detective for that, Frank, not me."

"If that's what you think, then you hire him," Frank said, "but I want you takin' care of this for me, Eddie. You pay the detective, and I'll pay you."

I figured this must be a pretty good friend of his if he was willing to foot the bill.

"Who recommended me for this?"

"Nobody recommended you for this specific job because I haven't told anybody about it," Frank said. "I haven't even told you the whole story, yet. But Jack speaks very highly of you, and I asked around. Your name always comes up when I tell people I need something done in Vegas. 'Get Eddie G,' they say, so I got you. Now ask me the other question you wanna ask."

"The other question?"

"The obvious one."

"Oh," I said, "who is this friend of yours whose life's been threatened?"

Frank pointed at me.

"Me?"

"On your back, pally," he said, and I realized he was pointing to the robe I was wearing. "The Dago."

"Dean?" I asked. "Dean Martin is the man we're talkin' about?"

"That's right," he said, "Dino."

"Why would somebody threaten Dean Martin's life?" I asked.

"Who knows why a wacko does what he does?" Frank asked. "If they were threatenin' Sammy I'd say it's because he was black, or a Jew, or both. Joey? Maybe somebody don't like his jokes. But Dean? He's a pussycat. Everybody loves the guy."

"Not everybody, I guess."

"No, you're right," he said, "not everybody." He leaned forward, put his hands on his bony knees. I always wondered what Ava Gardner saw in the guy, but let me tell you, up close, when you're in the same room with him, he's got something. It worked on women better than on men, but it was still there. Sex appeal. Charisma. Whatever you wanted to call it. It made women love him, and men want to be his friend.

"Look," he said, "we're filmin' this picture here in town."

"Right, *Ocean's Eleven*," I said. "Everybody knows about it."

"Yeah, well that's probably part of the problem. Too damn many people know about it. We got a three-week shoot on this thing, startin' tomorrow."

"Why don't you put it off until you can find out who's sendin' the threats?"

"Can't," Frank said, "it'd cost too much money."

"Then why not give Dean some time off, shoot around him?" I asked. "You do that sometimes in the movies, right? Shoot around somebody?"

"Yeah we do it," Frank said, "and I've suggested it to him, but he won't have it. He's not takin' these threats serious enough."

"But you are?"

"I've had death threats, pally," Frank said, "and you don't want to know who from. They're no fun, and a lot of the times they're serious." He picked up a towel that was sitting on the riser next to him and I saw a .38 Smith & Wesson. He dropped the towel back down. Now I knew why there was a shoulder holster hanging on a peg outside. I wondered if the steam was bad for the gun. "I pack heat wherever I go now. And yeah, I got a license for it."

"Why not go to the police?'

"Publicity," Frank said. "I know, you're thinking that there's no bad publicity. If it was me I'd go to the cops and let it get out, but Dean's a private person. He's not like me. He doesn't want to go to the police."

"Does he know you're talkin' to me?"

"No," Frank said. "If he knew he'd take my head off."

"Well then, how can I help him?"

"You come to the show tonight," Frank said. "Joey'll give you tickets. Bring a dame. After the show Joey'll take you to Dean's suite. Once you're there he won't toss you out. He's too much of a gentleman."

"I get to meet Dean Martin?"

Frank regarded me with an amused look on his face.

"So you're a fan?"

"Well . . . yeah . . ."

"Don't be embarrassed," Frank said. "I'm a big fan of Dino's, too. He's the real deal. I may be a crooner, but he's a singer. He's got the pipes."

I was surprised to hear Frank talk that way about somebody else.

As if reading my mind Frank said, "Does that surprise you, to hear me talk that way about Dean?"

"I didn't mean—"

"Hey, relax," Frank said. "Dean doesn't have a bigger fan than me. He's so cool he doesn't care about all this." He waved his hands to encompass—I assumed—all of Las Vegas. "He's only doin' the movie as a favor to me. That's why I want to help him, why I want you to help him."

"Frank," I said, groping for the right words, "I'll do what I can."

It sounded lame to me, but apparently it was what Frank wanted to hear.

"Hey," he said, "that's all I'm askin'."

# Five

I LEFT THE STEAM ROOM before Frank, feeling like a dried out prune. I don't know how he could spend so much time in there, but it may have had something to do with his being so thin—or cool. I replaced Dean's robe and took a quick shower before getting dressed.

When I got back to the casino floor I didn't see Joey anywhere. Instead of looking for him, I went to the bar and ordered a cold beer, to replace some of the fluids I'd lost in the Rat Pack steam room.

A hand fell on my shoulder from behind and Joey Bishop said, "There you are."

He took the stool next to me.

"Drink?" I asked.

"Not for me," he said, smiling. "Where do we stand?"

"You're supposed to give me a ticket to tonight's show."

"How about two?" he asked, plucking them from his pocket.

"That'll be fine." I grabbed them and put them in my breast pocket, then had some more beer. I checked my watch. I needed a change of clothes and a second, more thorough shower. Luckily, I'd be able to do that without leaving the hotel, one of the perks of being a pit boss, and somebody Jack Entratter—usually—liked.

"Well," Joey said, "I'll see you after the show and we'll go to Dean's suite."

"Hey, hey," I said, turning in my stool and grabbing his arm, "what's the story between Frank and Dean?"

"Truthfully?"

"Yeah, truthfully."

He settled back onto his stool.

"You tell anybody I told you this and I'll deny it."

"Agreed."

Joey took a moment to form his thoughts.

"Frank and Dean are two very different people," he said, finally. "Frank likes to surround himself with people who need him. Dean doesn't need anybody. He's very secure in who he is."

"And Frank's not?"

"Don't put words in my mouth," Joey warned. "Just let me tell it."

"Sorry."

"The truth of the matter is Frank has wanted to be Dean's friend since he first met him. He thinks Dean is the coolest cat he knows. Personally, I agree. As for Dean—well, he's Dean. Talk to him about being part of this Rat Pack and he can take it or leave it."

"And the rest of you?"

Joey hesitated, then said, "Let's just say that Dean is the only one who doesn't absolutely need Frank on some level."

I figured that was fair. I couldn't really expect Joey Bishop to say that Joey Bishop needed Frank Sinatra. But I thought pretty much anyone who paid attention to the news knew what Peter Lawford brought to the table. Personally, while Dean Martin was the one I wanted to meet, I thought Sammy Davis Jr. had the most talent. Unfortunately, there were things in Sammy's life that held him back. He probably needed Frank in order to get around those things.

But I wasn't really interested in the inner workings of the Pack. I was concerned with the Sinatra/Martin relationship.

"So Frank and Dean are friends?"

"Frank and Dean are good friends," Joey said.

"That's what I wanted to know."

"Then I'm out of here," Joey said, getting down from his stool. "I've got to get ready for the show. Meet me backstage when it's over, okay?"

"Okay."

Joey waved and left the bar. I was finishing the last of my beer when Beverly sidled up next to me.

"You gettin' friends in high places, Eddie?" she asked.

I turned and looked at her. She was a redhead in her thirties, and fit her Sands uniform very nicely. She probably didn't have the legs to be a showgirl, but she sure had everything else. Her red hair seemed natural, her green eyes sparkled, and she had full, kissable lips. I knew from other conversations that she was the sole support of a kid, although I didn't know if it was a boy or girl, or how old the child was.

I slid the two tickets from my pocket and said, "How would you like to go to a Rat Pack show with me tonight, doll?"

"Really?" She sighed and her eyes got wide. "I love Frank Sinatra."

"Have you been to see the show?"

"I haven't had the time," she said, "or the money—not for tickets, and not for a babysitter."

"Well, I've got the tickets," I said, waving them, "and I'll pay for the babysitter. Whataya say?"

"Eddie," she said, breathlessly. "I don't know what to say."

I looked down at the creamy white of her swelling cleavage and replied, "Please say yes."

She took a deep breath—which inflated her cleavage even more—and said, "Yes!"

# *Six*

DEAN MARTIN PICKED Sammy Davis Jr. up, walked to the microphone with him and said, "I want to thank the NAACP for this award." The audience—and Sammy—cracked up.

Frank, Dean, Sammy, Joey and Peter sang, danced, joked, did impressions (Sammy), smoked, stood around (Lawford) and the crowd loved it. This was Frank's "Summit of Cool," as he called it, because during that same month Eisenhower, de Gaulle and Khrushchev were having their summit conference in Paris.

Beverly hung on my arm and released it only to clap her hands together gleefully at the Rat Pack's on-stage antics. She was also excited to see some of the celebrities in the audience, specifically some of the other players in *Ocean's 11* like Angie Dickinson, Henry Silva and Richard Conte who, I later learned, was called "Nick" by Dean and other friends.

When the show was over I leaned over and whispered in Beverly's ear, "I have to go back stage. Would you like to come?"

"Oh, my God!" she said, which I took as a yes.

There was a security force to keep the Rat Packers safe—Frank alone had eight guards. I wondered if he was sharing them with Dean. All I had to do was give my name to one and he allowed us to go backstage, where it was already crowded with celebrity well-wishers and hangers-on.

Booze flowed freely, and I saw Frank standing in a corner with a brunette stunner named Judith Campbell on his arm. I was able to introduce Bev formally to Joey Bishop, and then said to Joey, "Bev would love to meet Frank and Dean."

"Dean's already gone up to his suite," Joey said, "but we can do Frank."

Joey tugged us over to where Frank was holding court with Henry Silva and Nick Conte. I looked around, but Angie Dickinson was nowhere to be seen. She had been the one I wanted to meet. I wanted to see if she was as sexy off-screen as on. Maybe another time . . .

"Frank," I said, as he looked at me, "the show was great."

"Who's the pretty lady, Eddie?" Frank asked, and I felt Bev's nails dig into my arm.

"Frank Sinatra," I said, "meet Beverly Carter."

"It's my pleasure," Frank said, graciously. He took Bev's hand and kissed it. He didn't bother to introduce Judith Campbell to either of us, and the buxom brunette stood there staring daggers at the equally buxom Beverly, who didn't notice at all. She only had eyes for Frank.

"Hey, Frank," Henry Silva said with a rakish smile, "this redhead's a knockout. You should give her a part in the film." Silva had two young dolls hanging off each arm. I later found they were conventioneering teachers he had plucked from the audience.

"Are you an actress, sweetheart?" Frank asked Bev.

"No," Bev said, "I'm just a waitress in the lounge, Mr. Sinatra."

"Hmph," Judith said, "a waitress."

"Would you like to be in a movie, Beverly?" Frank asked.

"Oh my God," Beverly said.

"Frank—" Judith said.

"Quiet, Judy," Frank told her. "Joey, why don't you take Eddie to his meeting? Eddie, leave Beverly here with us. We'll take good care of her."

"Shall we go?" Joey asked.

"I'll be back soon," I said to Bev, but I didn't think she heard me.

As I followed Joey across the crowded room I heard Frank say, "Bev, meet my good friend Nick Conte . . ."

"Might lose your girl to Frank or Nick tonight, Eddie," Joey said, as we left the Copa Room and reentered the hotel.

"She's not my girl, Joey," I said. "I just invited her along because you gave me two tickets."

"Hey, you could do worse," he said, with a shrug, "She's a beauty."

"Yes," I said, "she is."

Actually, I couldn't help but *be* a little miffed about losing Bev to the *Ocean's 11* crowd, but what could I do about it? I had also wanted to meet Sammy Davis Jr., who had been talking to some people in another part of the room with Peter Lawford, but that didn't happen that night, either.

As we rode the elevator up Joey said, "You're gonna meet Mack Gray, first."

"Who's he?"

"His real name is Maxie Greenberg, but everybody calls him Mack Gray. He's an old-time fight manager who ended up bein' George Raft's personal assistant for years. When Raft fell on hard times and couldn't afford Mack anymore he passed him on to Dean. See, Dean sort of idolized George Raft when he was comin' up in the business. Rather than letting Mack go altogether George convinced Dean to give him a job doin' the same sort of things he did for Raft. So now Mack is Dean's personal assistant. Mack and Jay Girard also act as a sort of buffer between Dino and the outside world."

I found out later that Jay Girard—real name "Girardi"—was, for a long time, Dean's stand-in and went on to become a sort of Man Friday for him. It seemed to me Dean Martin was pretty loyal to his friends.

"Is Raft in *Ocean's Eleven*?' I asked Joey.

"Dean got him a small part," Joey said. "Now there's a cool cat."

Joey was right. Because of Dean's facade of cool I was surprised to learn that he had ever idolized anyone—but not surprised that it was George Raft. Raft, even to this day when he wasn't working all that much, still epitomized cool.

The elevator doors opened and Joey said, "Come on. Dean's gonna want to turn in soon."

"No parties?" I asked, following him down the hall.

"Dean's not the partier everybody thinks he is. He actually likes to go to sleep fairly early."

"I didn't know that about him."

When we reached the door Joey said, "You're about to find out a lot of things about Dean Martin that nobody knows."

# Seven

Mack Gray opened the door and let us in. He was wearing an expensive suit and a white shirt.

"Mack, meet Eddie Gianelli," Joey said. "Eddie, Mack Gray."

Gray closed the door then turned and looked at me.

"This the clyde who's supposed to help the boss?" he asked.

"Clyde" was Rat Pack-ese for anyone who wasn't part of their group.

"This is him. Say hello, Mack."

Mack regarded me for a moment from on high—he was taller than me by several inches—and then stuck out his big hand. We shook briefly, and he stared at me like I was a puzzle he was trying to figure out. Actually, he was frowning as if something hurt him.

"Mack?" Joey said.

"Huh?" He had the fingertips of his right hand pressed to his forehead.

"Dean?"

"He's gettin' changed," Mack said. "I'll go and tell him yer here."

Mack disappeared down a hall, leaving us in a plushly furnished living room.

"Either he doesn't like me or he's got a headache."

"Probably both," Joey said. "Mack suffers from migraine headaches. Nothin' seems to help, but he pops Percodan like they were M&M's."

There was a bar against one wall which looked fully stocked, with a refrigerator behind it. A beautiful three-cushion burgundy sofa with two matching armchairs. In front of the sofa was a rectangular coffee table covered with comic books. I looked at Joey, who smiled.

"Dean likes to read comic books."

"Why?"

Joey shrugged. "He says they help him escape from reality."

I leaned over and leafed through them. Superman, Batman and other superheroes. He wasn't hiding them, so he wasn't ashamed of reading them. That sort of went hand in hand with Dean being cool, if you thought about it.

"Eddie," Joey said, "I'm gonna leave you alone here."

"Alone? With Dean?"

Joey laughed. "Don't worry. He's not gonna bite you. You weren't this nervous about meeting Frank."

"Well . . . I'm a big Dino fan."

"I see. Frank must have appreciated that, since he's a big Dean fan, too."

"So he said."

"Is that why you agreed to help, finally?" Joey asked. "When you heard it was Dean who needed the help?"

"Joey," I said, "I went to the meeting with Frank because Jack Entratter told me to."

"And what about now? Frank didn't tell you to talk to Dean, did he?"

"No," I said, "he asked me to, and he told me to feel free to say no."

"But you didn't."

"For two reasons," I said. "One, if I said no I'd pay for it one way or another, and two, like I said, I'm a big fan. It's a chance for me to meet Dean. And if I can help him, I will."

"Okay." He looked at his watch. "I gotta go. Maybe I'll see you tomorrow."

"Joey—"

He turned as he reached the door. "Don't worry, you'll be fine."

And he left. I was standing alone in the living room of Dean Martin's suite, not sure what to do with myself. I was impressed to meet Frank Sinatra, but this . . . this was different for me. I had a shitload of Dean Martin records at home, and never missed any of his movies. In my humble opinion, his split with Jerry Lewis was the best thing that had ever happened to him. *The Young Lions, Some Came Running,* and the more recent *Rio Bravo* proved his acting ability, and his recordings proved what a great singer he was. Even before Joey told me, I always had the feeling Dean didn't need Frank. He didn't need to make a movie like *Ocean's 11,* he simply wanted to. He did not need a career boost from Frank Sinatra. Dean Martin out-cooled them all—Sinatra, Sammy . . . hell, even George Raft.

I heard somebody coming down the hall and turned to see Mack returning.

"Dean'll be out in a minute," he said in a monotone. He still had his hand pressed to his head, this time the heel. "He said you should help yourself to a drink if you want."

He headed for the door.

"You're not staying, Mack?"

He turned, dropped his hand and glared at me.

"I ain't been invited to stay," he said, and left. The big man's feelings may have really been hurt, but that wasn't my problem. I wondered if he had any idea what was going on, or if Dean was keeping it from him? I also wondered if Joey knew what the problem was, or Sammy and Peter, for that matter.

I went over to the bar and looked it over, but nothing appealed to me until I opened the refrigerator and found it stocked with beer. There were enough brands in there for a variety of tastes and I finally chose a can of Piels. I found a can opener and had it ready to use when Dean Martin came down the hall and into the living room.

He was wearing a yellow polo shirt with a white collar, light gray slacks and a pair of black loafers. His hair was wet, so he had probably showered after the show. I stood rooted behind the bar, because when I woke up that morning I had never expected to be in the same room as Dean Martin. He walked over to the bar and extended his right hand, after shifting his cigarette to his left.

"Eddie?" he said. "I'm Dean Martin."

I shook his hand and said, "I know. I saw the show tonight."

"Did ya, now?" he asked. He shifted the cigarette back to his right hand, holding it between his forefinger and middle finger. "What'd you think?"

"It was . . . entertaining." That sounded lame, even to me.

"Entertaining," he repeated. "Well, I guess that's what we want, eh?"

"I mean . . . it was great. You and Frank and Sammy, you're great entertainers."

"Ah," Dean said, "alone, we're great entertainers. When we get together we're a bunch of clowns—but hey, the people loved it, right?"

"They did," I agreed. "They loved it."

Dean sat on a bar stool and faced me.

"Why don't you get me something to drink, if you don't mind, since you're already behind the bar?"

"Sure, Mr. Martin," I said, "what'll it be?"

"First," he said, "call me Dean, and second, just get me a bottle of soda water out of the refrigerator, and a glass of ice."

"Oh, uh, right."

I'd expected him to ask for gin or bourbon, but I filled a glass with ice and took a bottle of water from the fridge. I opened it and poured it for him, and left the bottle on the bar.

"Thanks, pally," he said, and took a generous swallow. He sucked the cigarette to death and stubbed it out in a heavy glass ashtray.

"So you talked to Frank," he said. "He gave you the run down?"

"He only told me that you were gettin' death threats, Mist—uh, Dean. Nothing more than that."

"I'm not sure there is anything more than that," Dean said, "but Frank's worried. When Frank worries everybody tends to worry."

"Well, how many people know about these threats?"

"So far," Dean said, "you, me and Frank."

"Not Mack?"

"Mack doesn't need to know. He'd mother-hen me to death, and he'd give himself an ulcer to go along with his headaches."

"Seems to me he left with his feelings hurt."

"Mack'll get over it."

"What about Joey?"

"He doesn't know the particulars, either," Dean said. "Frank just used him to get you involved."

"Don't you think you should tell the folks who are involved with the movie? The director? The producer? The other actors?"

"Eddie," Dean said, "I'm not absolutely convinced that there is really something to the threats. Why raise the alarm without knowing?"

"And you want me to find out?"

"Frank tells me you know everybody in town," Dean said. "You could make some discreet inquiries."

"To tell you the truth, Dean," I said, "I don't know exactly what I can do, but I'm willing to try to help."

"That's fine," Dean said. "I appreciate that. Just no police, and no reporters. Not yet, anyway."

"All right, then," I said, "I suppose we should start with the threats. How did you get them?"

"Just a minute."

Dean got off his stool, walked to a writing desk at the far end of the room, and took some papers from a drawer. He brought them back to the bar and put them down in front of me. I spread them out and saw that they were letters—notes, really. Half a dozen of them.

YOU AIN'T TOO BIG TO GET HURT one of them said. Another went IF YOU'RE NOT CAREFUL YOU COULD GET REAL HURT. Some of the others were more to the point about what the injuries could be.

"They're printed," I said, "in block letters. Hard to identify handwriting from that."

"I know," Dean said.

"And I get the feeling the person who wrote these isn't very educated." I looked at him. "Do you suspect anyone, Dean?"

"I can't really think of anybody who'd want to harm me."

"What about somebody who maybe just wants to scare you?"

"For what reason?"

"I don't know," I said. "You're rich, handsome, famous, maybe somebody's jealous. Somebody you stepped on gettin' to where you are now."

That annoyed Dean. He pushed away from the bar and paced the room.

"I never stepped on anybody in my life," he said. "I worked hard getting where I am."

"Well, then maybe it's somebody who's jealous of you, simply because you're you."

"That's crazy."

"Well, it's got to be someone," I said. "We've got the notes to prove that." I spread the papers out. "Where are the envelopes they came in?"

"I threw them out, I guess."

"They came in the regular mail? Or were they delivered by messenger?" I was running out of questions. Not being a cop or a private eye, I wasn't sure what else to ask.

Dean thought a moment, then said, "Regular mail. They had stamps on them."

"Okay," I said, "if you get anymore I guess you should keep the envelopes."

"They didn't have any return address on them."

"What about postmarks?" I asked. "Were they mailed from here in Las Vegas? Were the stamps even canceled?"

Dean's shoulders slumped.

"I didn't notice," he said. "That was stupid."

"Never mind," I said. "Just remember with the next one . . . if there is a next one."

I wasn't sure what to ask him next, but the guy looked so disheartened, I didn't want to leave yet.

Suddenly, he asked, "Where are you from?"

"New York," I said, "Brooklyn."

"When did you leave?"

"About twelve years ago."

"I worked hard to get the Ohio out of my tone," he said. "I always thought it was part of the reason I succeeded."

"Could be,"

"Why would someone want to hurt me," he asked, abandoning the small talk, "or threaten to hurt me just because I succeeded?"

"Success is somethin' to envy, Dean," I said, "and, for some people, somethin' to resent."

"I suppose you're right." He looked at his watch. "There's an old John Wayne film on the television in five minutes. Ever since we did *Rio Bravo* together I try to catch all his early movies. Want to stay and watch?"

What an invitation! Any other time I would have jumped at the chance to watch television with Dean Martin in his room.

"I think I better get started on this, Dean," I said. "I'd like to find out right away whether I can help or not. I don't wanna waste your time."

"My time, pally?" Dean asked. "I got nothin' but time to waste. It's your time you'll be wastin'. I hope we're payin' you enough."

"You're not paying me at all," I said. "This is a favor all the way down the line."

Dean regarded me for a moment, then stuck out his hand and said, "Thanks, Eddie. I really appreciate it."

I shook hands with him and said, "I'll be in touch."

When I left the room he was turning on the TV to watch John Wayne. I hoped the movie would take his mind off the threats that were obviously bothering him more than he let on.

# Eight

I WENT STRAIGHT HOME that night after my meeting with Dean because I had no idea where Bev had gone. It was a good bet she was with Frank and Nick and Henry and the *Ocean's 11* crowd. Since this had been our first "date" and we'd had no previous relationship beyond waitress and customer—and two employees of the Sands—I wasn't really that upset about it. I might have been worried, but I'd left her in the care of Frank Sinatra. Or maybe I should have been worried *because* I'd left her in his care. Whatever the case, when I couldn't find her or Joey Bishop, or anyone else connected to the Rat Pack, I went home.

I lived just far enough off the strip so I couldn't see the bright lights. That was actually as far from it as I wanted to be, because I drew energy from the lights and activity of Las Vegas. I knew some folks who worked for the casinos and stayed far away from them when they weren't working. You could often find me on the strip, in the casinos, in my off hours. I didn't gamble as much as I used to, but I still liked to play some blackjack now and then—but never at the Sands. I didn't shit where I worked.

But this night I decided to have a drink in the privacy of my own living room and think about the events of the day. Meeting two of the most famous men in the world, Frank Sinatra and Dean Martin. Nothing could have prepared me for that.


I got up the next morning and went out for breakfast after making a phone call. When I got to the Sands coffee shop I found Danny Bardini waiting for me.

Danny and I grew up together in Brooklyn and ended up in Vegas. He came a few years after I did, and had to quit working for the New York cops to do it. Me, all I'd left behind was a job as an accountant. Being good with numbers was what made me a good card player. He came out to Vegas, got a P.I. ticket and had been keyhole-peeping his way to wealth ever since. We shook hands, and he bruised me with a big, shiny diamond pinky ring.

"Breakfast at the Sands on you?" he said. "Must be something you need, bad, for you to call me on short notice."

"You came, didn't you? On short notice?"

"Hey," he said, "I love ya, Eddie. Why wouldn't I leave a warm bed with an even warmer broad in it to have breakfast with you?"

"Let's get seated and I'll tell you a story."

We got a table easily and both ordered steak and eggs. Danny was a few years younger than I was. Actually, back in Brooklyn his older brother, Nick, had been my best friend. When Nick was killed in a gang fight I sort of took Danny under my wing, until he joined the police department and had plenty of new brothers in blue. That's when we sort of went our separate ways until we met up again in Vegas.

When we had coffee in front of us Danny said, "Okay, so tell me a story."

I did, starting with Joey, moving onto Frank and then, finally, Dean. I threw Jack Entratter in there for good measure.

Danny's eyes were wide when I finished and he said, "You got to meet Dean Martin?"

"That's the little picture, Danny," I said. "Take a look at the big picture."

"Hey," Danny said, "for me that is the big picture. Did you see Angie Dickinson?"

"Only in the audience."

"Hey, what happened to Bev—"

"Big picture, Danny," I said, "I need you to look at the big picture."

"Okay," Danny said, "okay, somebody's threatenin' Dean Martin. Is that unusual? Don't Hollywood types get threats all the time?"

"I suppose they do, but Frank Sinatra seems to think there's something to this one."

"Well," Danny said, pushing his nose to one side, "if Frank thinks so why doesn't he get some help from the boys?"

"Look," I said, "Jack asked me to help Frank, Frank asked me to help Dean—"

"Geez," Danny said, as the waiter appeared, "you're turnin' into some helluva name-dropper."

I waited for the waiter to leave and then leaned forward.

"I need your help, Danny. I'm not sure how to go about this."

"Eddie," he said, around a mouthful of steak and eggs, "I peek through peepholes. What do I know about death threats?"

"Look," I said, "between you and me we got this town wired, don't we?"

"That's true."

"We know everybody."

"Just about."

"So between us we can find out what's going on."

Now it was Danny's turn to lean forward.

"If I help with this do I get to meet Dean Martin?" he asked.

"I'll arrange it."

"And Angie Dickinson?"

"I'll work on it."

"Are we gettin' paid for this gig?"

"Not a cent."

"Geez, we're a couple of swell guys, huh?"

"Dean Martin, Danny," I said. "Remember?"

"I gotcha," he said. "Tell me about the threats."

"I left the notes with Dean," I said, "but some of them were pretty fuckin' graphic."

"They come in the mail?"

"Yes."

"Postmarks?"

"I don't have the envelopes."

I gave him everything Dean had told me about the notes, which admittedly wasn't much.

"Boy, you don't want much for steak and eggs, do ya?" he asked. "There ain't much to go on here, Eddie."

"I know it," I said, "but how was I supposed to say no to Dean Martin and Frank Sinatra?"

"Good point."

We finished our breakfast and were on our last cup of coffee when Danny looked up and his eyes widened.

"You sleep with anybody's wife lately?"

"Not so far this week," I said. "Why?"

"There's a kinda angry lookin', um, big guy makin' his way towards us."

I turned in my seat and saw Mack Gray knock a waiter out of his way as he continued his path to our table.

"Who is this guy?"

"Mack Gray," I said. "He works for Dean Martin."

"Am I gonna have to shoot him?"

"Do you have your gun with you?"

"No."

"Then what's the difference? Let's just see what he wants before we panic."

"He looks real mad," Danny said. "You can wait if you want, but I'm gonna panic now."

When Mack Gray reached our table he stopped and glared down at me.

"You an' me gotta talk, Clyde."

"Mr. Gray," I said, "meet my friend, Danny Bardini."

"How are ya?" Danny asked. He didn't offer to shake hands, just kept his fork in one hand and his steak knife in the other.

"Take a walk," Gray said.

"Eddie?" Danny asked, looking very calm for a man who said he was panicking. "You want me to take a walk?"

"Why don't you start workin' on what we talked about, Danny," I said, "and I'll find out what Mack wants."

"Okay." Danny stood up and stared at Mack Gray, who glared back. "Nice to meet you, pal."

Gray pushed out his jaw, but then revealed he wasn't as hard and tough as he liked to make out he was when he said, "Yeah, likewise."

Danny looked at me, raised his eyebrows and left.

"Sit down, Mack," I said. "I'll buy you a cup of coffee."

# Nine

I WANNA KNOW what's goin' on," Mack Gray said to me, after sitting down but refusing coffee.

"Ask Dean."

"He ain't talkin'."

"Well, then I can't, either, Mack. If Dean wanted you to know, he'd've told you."

Mack slammed his fist down on the table, rattling everything around us and attracting attention. It was like a small earthquake. He had a pained look on his face.

"Mack—" I said, warily.

"This ain't right." Mack pressed the fingers of one hand to his head. "I been with him for eight years. He shouldn't keep anything from me."

"Maybe he's got his reasons, Mack," I said. "Maybe he's—"

Abruptly, he got up and walked off, leaving me in mid-sentence. I understood he felt hurt, maybe even a little betrayed, but it wasn't my place to tell him anything.

I paid for breakfast and left the restaurant. I did not have the day off, but I wondered if I could have—and more?

\* \* \*

Jack Entratter regarded me from behind his desk and a fat cigar. "So you've got a job to do for Frank?"

"More like a favor for Frank, and for Dean Martin, Jack," I said.

"What's it about?"

I hesitated, then said, "I think that would be better coming from Frank or Dean."

Entratter took the cigar out of his mouth and peered at me through a haze of blue smoke.

"You work for me, son," he said. "Don't forget that."

"I won't, Jack," I said, "but it's my guess you want to keep Frank and Dean happy, right?"

"Well . . . yeah . . ."

"Then I've got to keep their confidence," I asked. "Don't I?"

He stuck the cigar back in his face and sat back in his chair.

"You're a smartass, Eddie," he said. "That's probably why I like you—but don't push it."

"Look," I said, checking my watch, "I have to go to work, so I won't be able to do anything for Frank or Dean until—"

"Whoa," he said, holding up his hand. "Didn't we just talk about keeping them happy?"

"Well, yeah, but I've still got a job—"

"You're off the clock," Entratter said, "as of now. Got it?"

"Well, sure, Jack," I said. "That's real nice of you to offer—"

"Offer, my ass," he said, "That's what you came in here to get, only you wanted me to think it was my idea, right?"

I guess I looked a bit sheepish then.

"I said you were a smartass, Eddie," he said, "I didn't say you were smarter than me. Understand?"

"I understand, Jack."

"Now get outta here."

I stood up to leave.

"One more thing," he said, before I got to the door.

"What's that, Jack?"

"You report to me at the end of each day," he said. "I wanna know what's goin' on."

"I think I can do that."

"If you can't," he said, "you better have a good reason why. *Capice?*"

Jack Entratter wasn't Italian, and that was one of the only words he knew.

"*Capice*, Jack."

# Ten

I WASN'T USED TO BEING a free man, with time on my hands. Not having to go to work that day left me feeling curiously empty. I loved my job, loved the feel of a busy casino, especially one as large and bustling as the Sands.

But there were other casinos that basically offered the same things. If I stepped out onto the strip I could turn left and walk to Bugsy Siegel's place, the Flamingo, or to the right to the Desert Inn or, beyond that, the Thunderbird.

My personal favorite—other than the Sands—was the Flamingo. I think it was because of the history. It was, after all, the casino that had started it all.

But I didn't have time to go casino-hopping. I decided to go to the bar to do some thinking over a drink. It was early in the day to start, but then I didn't have to be at work anytime soon. When I got there I saw that Bev was working. I grabbed a barstool rather than sit at a table.

"A little early for you, ain't it, Eddie?" the bartender asked.

"No harm getting an early start once in a while, is there, Harry?"

"Hell, no. What'll be?"

"Bourbon, rocks."

"Comin' up."

When he had me set up, Beverly came sidling up next to me.

"Well, what happened to you, last night?"

"I might ask you the same thing."

"After you abandoned me," she said, "Frank and Henry asked me to go out with them."

"And Miss Campbell?"

Bev made a face. "She didn't want me to go."

"She was jealous of you."

"I didn't take that as a compliment," she said. "She'd be jealous of any woman."

"You could have gone with them as Henry Silva's date, though."

She laughed. "He already had three women. I think that was enough for him to handle."

"So what did you do?"

"I went home. I waited a while for you to come back, and then I went home."

"Alone?"

"What do you mea—"

"I just meant," I said, hurriedly, "that nobody put you in a cab, or anything?"

"Actually," she said, "Nick Conte walked me to the door and saw me into a cab—and he was a complete gentleman."

I felt foolish for thinking she'd gone out on the town with the Rat Pack.

"I'm sorry, Bev," I said. "I had to go up and see Dean Martin."

Her eyes widened. "You're friends with Dean Martin?"

"Well not exactly," I said. "I had some business with him."

"What kind of business?"

"The kind I can't talk about," I said.

"I'm impressed," she said. "At least you abandoned me for a good reason."

"I didn't abandon—"

"I'm kidding, Eddie."

"I came down and looked for you, but you'd gone by that time. I guess it wasn't much of a date, was it?"

"Is that what it was?" she said. "A date?"

"Well . . . wasn't it?"

She thought a moment, then said, "I suppose it was—and as first dates go, it was a doozy."

"I know," I said, "I'm sorry—"

"No," she said, "I meant that in a good way. I had a good time, I really did. The show was hysterical. I think I'd rather hear Frank and Dean sing—and Sammy Davis, too—but it was fun."

"It was?"

"You know how to show a girl a good time, Eddie," she said. "I mean, taking me backstage to meet all those famous people? It was a great date, believe me."

"Uh, well, I'm glad," I said. "I'm real glad you enjoyed it, Bev."

"Do me a favor?"

"Anything."

"Ask me out again, some time?"

"Well . . . of course. I mean, for this to have been a first date there'd have to be a second, right?"

"And next time I'll let you see me home," she promised.

"It's a deal. Thanks, Bev."

"No," she said, "thank you, Eddie."

She turned and flounced away, knowing I was watching. Her walk was something to behold.

# Eleven

I WAS STILL SITTING on the stool, nursing the same drink, when Joey Bishop entered the bar. He spotted me and came walking over with a spring in his step.

"You look happy," I said.

"I'm always happy after a good show," he said. "Last night was a good show."

"What happened to you after?" I asked. "Did you go out with the rest of 'em?"

"I turned in," Joey said. "I can't handle the nightlife like Frank and Peter and Sammy can. How about you? How did your meeting with Dean go?'

"Fine, I guess."

"Are you, uh, helping him out?"

"I am," I said. "You got any idea what it's about, Joey?"

"No," he said, "but if Frank or Dean want me to know, they'll tell me."

"Fair enough," I said, "but tell me more about Mack Gray?"

"Mack? What about him?"

"That's what I'm asking you."

"He's a loyal guy," Joey said. "He was loyal to George Raft for years, and now he's loyal to Dean."

"Why would Dean keep anything from him, then?"

"I don't know, Eddie," Joey said. "You'd have to ask Dean. Why? Did Mack say anything to you?"

"Mack is mad," I said, "I'm just not sure if he's mad at me or at Dean."

"Mack doesn't get mad at Dean, ever," Joey said.

"Great, then he's mad at me. I don't need that."

"If you want Mack off your back go to Dean," Joey said. "He'll take care of it."

"No, I'll wait a while," I said. "I don't wanna bother Dean until I have something positive to tell him."

"Well," Joey said, slapping me on the back, "I saw you from across the floor and thought I'd ask you how things went."

"Can I buy you a drink?"

He shook his head. "I don't drink. One of these days we'll have coffee, or tea. I'll see ya."

I watched Joey go, wondering how he could hang out with those guys and remain a teetotaler?

Harry waved my money away for the drink, so I dropped a generous tip on the bar and left.


I spent time talking to some of the Sands employees who might have known or seen something. I also spoke with the front desk and security staff about mail practices in the hotel. Who got it, who delivered it, that sort of thing. After that I talked with the people who really run Vegas—the bellmen and the valets. I asked whatever questions came to mind, collected information and stored it away in my head. Once I was finished talking with staff at the Sands, I knew I was going to have to spend some time outside the casino. I had contacts in all the other casinos, but I couldn't just put out word that I was looking for someone who had been heard threatening Dean Martin. That would have been something less than discreet. So instead of simply "putting the word out," I was going to have to do some pavement-pounding and talk to my contacts individually. Some were merely contacts but others were also friends, so I would have to deal with each of them on a very individual basis.

It was going to take quite a bit of time.

By the time I got home that night my feet hurt from the walking and I had a buzz on because a lot of the conversations had taken place over drinks. If I hadn't been just a little bit looped I might have noticed that I had entered my own home without using the key. That might have alerted me that the scene was wrong, and helped me avoid a lot of pain.

As it was something hit me in the middle of the back just as I entered. The force of the blow propelled me forward awkwardly until I lost my balance and tumbled to the floor. I tried to catch my breath as the door slammed, and then the lamp clicked on.

In the dim light by the sofa I saw two men staring down at me. The blow had come not from a fist but from a blackjack one of them was holding. I had the feeling that he had not missed one of my kidneys by accident.

"Get his wallet," one of them said, as I still struggled to catch my breath. A shot to the middle of the back takes all the air out of your lungs and mine were screaming for a refill.

"What for?"

"I wanna see if he's the guy."

"He come walkin' in, didn't he?"

"The door wasn't locked."

"But he had a key in his hand," one of them said. "I heard it jingle."

"Get his fuckin' wallet, will ya?"

The guy without the blackjack reached down and lifted my wallet from my jacket. I couldn't have stopped him if I wanted to, but at least my breath was starting to come back. My eyes were tearing, though, so I couldn't see their faces clearly. The shadows thrown by the lamp didn't help matters any. Their faces were shrouded in it rather than illuminated.

"What's his name?" Blackjack asked.

"I'm lookin'," Wallet said. "Says on his driver's license 'Eddie Gianelli'?" He looked at his partner. "That the guy?"

"That's the guy."

My wallet came flying at me and landed on my chest.

"Whataya wanna do now?" the second man asked.

"Hold 'im down," Blackjack said. "I'm gonna hurt 'im."

"Hey," I finally managed to say, "what the hell—"

"Shut up," the second man said, and emphasized that this was an order and not a request with a kick to my ribs.

"We're only supposed to scare 'im, you know," he said to his partner.

"Yeah, well," Blackjack said, "hurtin' him will scare 'im, I guarantee ya. Just hold 'im."

The second guy got down behind me, then slid his arms inside my elbows and pulled my arms back, pinning them there with the aid of his knee, which he planted in my back right where the blackjack had hit me. It hurt so much I began to flail around, kicking my legs, until the man with the blackjack leaned down and rapped me on one knee with it. That made me forget the pain in my back as I howled.

"Hello?"

It was a woman's voice calling from the front door, which none of the three of us had heard open.

"We gotta go!" Blackjack hissed.

"Why?" the other man asked, almost in my ear. "It's just a broad."

"We got orders about him," the first man said, "not some broad. Let 'im go."

I felt my arms being released and I tried to shout a warning to whoever was at the door, but suddenly something hit me on the head and me and my tortured lungs went down a black hole . . .

# Twelve

HANDS WERE ON ME, shaking me.

"Eddie?"

The voice became insistent. It must not have been the first time she called my name.

"Come on, Eddie! Are you all right?"

The voice and the hands became more insistent.

"No," I said.

"Thank God."

I opened my eyes and looked up into the worried face of Dori Ellis, a showgirl who worked at the Sahara and, for the past few months, had been occasionally joining me in my bed.

"What happened?" she demanded. "Who were those guys?"

I peered up at her and realized I was seeing her with only one eye. There was something wet and sticky in my left one. I wiped at it with my hand, but that only made it worse.

"Oh, Jesus, you're bleeding," she said. "Are you all right?"

"Did they—did they hurt you?" I asked.

"No," she said, "they just pushed me aside and ran out of here. I guess I scared 'em."

"Help me up, Dori."

She got her arm under my shoulder and helped me to my feet. My knee screamed at me, my ribs ached, so did my back, and the wet, sticky stuff—my blood, I assumed—kept running down my face.

"Where to?" she asked.

"The sofa."

"You might bleed on it."

Just like a woman to worry about the furniture.

"I'll risk it."

With her help I limped to the sofa and dropped down onto it.

"Let me get something for your head," she said.

While she was gone I took inventory. Everything seemed to hurt, but nothing was broken. I swiped at the blood in my eye, smearing it all over my hand and face without clearing my vision. Dori returned with a wet washcloth and a couple of towels.

"Since you weren't worried about the sofa, I figured the same went for your towels," she said.

Gently she began washing blood from my face. At one point I took over so she wouldn't poke out my eyes trying to clean it. Once I could see I set the cloth aside and used a towel to wipe up the rest of the blood.

"Can you tell me what happened, now?" she asked.

"No," I said.

"Why not?"

"Because I don't know what happened," I said. "I walked in, I got hit, two guys started working me over and then you showed up. End of fuckin' story."

"Did they rob you. Did they get your wallet?"

"It should be on the floor over there somewhere."

She looked around, retrieved it for me and brought it over.

"Everything there?" she asked.

"Looks like it." I set the wallet aside.

"Did they say anything?"

"They argued a bit."

"Did they say anything to you?"

I thought a moment, then said, "Just shut up."

"That's odd," she said.

"Yeah, it is odd. Did they speak to you?"

"Well, yes," she said, "as they pushed me aside one of them said 'Tell your boyfriend to mind his own business.' What did he mean by that? Whose business have you been minding?"

"My own," I said, "and I don't usually have to be told to do it." I touched my knee and found it swollen, stretched it out to try and ease the pain. There didn't seem to be anything I could do for my back or my ribs.

"Your forehead is still bleeding," she said, pressing the second towel to it.

I reached up and put my hand on it so she could let go.

"I better call the police," she said.

"No—wait!"

She turned away from the phone and frowned at me. Dori was tall and statuesque, the way the casinos preferred their showgirls to be, and when she was all made up to go on stage she became beautiful. Freshly scrubbed the way she was now, though, she was simply achingly pretty.

"Why?"

"I need a minute to think."

I was still feeling disoriented from being attacked. Did I want the police called in? What could I tell them? I couldn't even describe the men.

"Would you be able to identify those two if you saw them again?" I asked.

"What? No, I don't think so. They went by me so fast, and shoved me out of the way . . ."

"Then I don't think it would do any good to call the police," I said. I was starting to think more clearly. What of this was connected to the threats on Dean Martin? After all, that was the only thing happening in my life that was out of the ordinary.

"Are you sleeping with somebody's wife, Eddie? Is that what this is about?"

Lately, we'd been having some problems and I'd started to think about ending our little arrangement—or what she had begun calling our "relationship."

"No, I haven't slept with anyone's wife, lately." Danny had asked me the same thing. When did I get that fuckin' reputation? "To tell you the truth, I don't know what this was all about, but they really seemed intent on hurting me."

"Maybe I should take you to the hospital?"

I leaned forward and reached behind me to rub my back. The blow had not landed on either of my kidneys, so I doubted I'd be pissing blood like a fighter after a bout. I probed my ribs, which didn't seem to be cracked. I'd had cracked ribs once before, so I knew from experience that it hurt like a bitch just to breathe. The worst problem seemed to be my knee, which had swelled up to about twice its size.

"I think some ice on my knee would be the best thing," I said. "How does my head look?"

I removed the towel so she could take a look. She took hold of my face and leaned me toward the light.

"One of the girls fell one night and hit her head. The doctor said scalp wounds bleed a lot, but aren't that serious. It doesn't look like you're going to need stitches."

"Okay, then," I said, "no cops and no doctors."

"But Eddie—"

She was wearing jeans and a man's shirt knotted below her large breasts. There was a considerable expanse of tummy showing, and I put my hand on her warm skin.

"I just think I need some tender loving care," I said.

"From me?" she asked, with a smile.

"You're the one who's here," I said, and then realized that may have been the wrong way to put it. "After all, you probably saved my life tonight. In some countries that makes you responsible for me."

"Eddie," she said, leaning forward so that her head came in contact with mine.

"Ow!" I said, and started bleeding again.

# Thirteen

I WOKE THE NEXT MORNING stiff and sore—but I was grateful to wake up, at all. If Dori hadn't come to the door, I might have been dead.

Dori stayed the night. She checked my eyes to make sure my pupils contracted in the light—she'd seen a doctor do this to the girl that had fallen onstage—and pronounced me concussion free.

We went to bed but didn't have sex. Not that I didn't want to. Dori's all woman, and having her next to me gave me a raging hard-on all night, but my aches and pains just wouldn't allow it. Believe me, we tried. The second time she whacked my sore knee with one of hers and we gave it up.

However, when we woke the next morning I was still hard, and she had pity on me.

Then she sprang a surprise on me while she was getting dressed.

"I think you should consider that a goodbye blowjob, Eddie."

"What?" I'd been distracted watching her move about the room naked, enjoying the play of her dancer's muscles beneath her smooth, pale skin.

"You've gotten yourself into something funny," she said, "and I don't mean 'ha ha' funny."

"Well," I said, "you're right about that." I watched as she fit her showgirl tits into her bra, then pulled on her top.

"Those men scared the shit out of me last night," she said, pulling on her panties and hip-huggers at the same time, "so now that I know you're all right I don't think I want to be around if and when they come back."

I couldn't blame her for that. They'd pretty much scared the shit out of me, too—which, according to one of them, had been their job. Hurting me, that just seemed to be something the first guy wanted to do because he liked it.

She put on her shoes, grabbed her purse and came over to the bed to kiss me goodbye.

"Give me a call when you've got it all sorted out," she said, then added, "then we'll see."

After she was gone I realized she'd been feeling the same thing I had, that maybe we'd run our course. We'd probably bump into each other around town—I'd even go to see her show—but we both knew that anything more than that was no longer an option.

In other words, we were done.


Being from Brooklyn I had seen a lot of street fights in my life. Hell, I had even done my time as a kid in a street gang, but had outgrown that stage very quickly. My point is I'm not really all that brave, but getting beat up didn't send me running right to the cops, either. In the light of day I decided not to bring them into it—at least, not until I talked to Dean, again.

I took a shower when I got up and then checked myself out in the mirror. None of my injuries were visible except for a bruised knee—and no one would see that once I got dressed. The wound on my scalp was covered by my hairline, at first glance no one could tell I'd been attacked. Probably the only explaining I'd have to do was about the slight limp. Good thing Dori and I had iced the knee the night before, or it would have been much worse come morning. It was still somewhat swollen, but not so bad I couldn't get my pants on. As far as the limp went, I was hoping that it would get stronger and start to handle all my weight as the day progressed.

I made myself some coffee and tried not to rub my knee while I drank it. There was nothing else going on in my life that would cause two men to break into my house, wait for me, and then try to hurt me. And "break" was not even the right word. There was no damage to my door, or to any of my windows. Those guys had gotten in slick as you please, which meant they were pros—and that meant they had probably been paid to do what they did—only they hadn't gotten the job done. Did that mean they'd be back? And wasn't that a good enough reason to call the police?

I was still going over the one hand and the other hand when the phone rang.

"Is this Eddie Gianelli?" a man's harsh voice asked. I didn't recognize it, but got a chill down my spine anyway. I had a feeling I knew why he was calling.

"That's right. What can I do for you?"

"Stay healthy, Eddie," the man said. "I can always send my friends back around.'

"Who is this?"

"That don't matter."

"Then what the fuck do you want?"

"Stick to what you know best," he said. "Don't be tryin' to branch out."

"What the hell are you talking about?"

"I'm talkin' about stickin' your nose where it don't belong," the man said. "I'm talkin' about doin' favors for people and gettin' hurt."

"You're talking about vague threats," I said, starting to get angry. "How am I supposed to know what you're warning me off of if you don't tell me?"

"Names don't matter," he said. "You got a job, do it. Just don't be freelancing, Eddie. It ain't healthy."

"For Chrissake," I yelled, "this isn't a Bogart movie, you stupid sonofa—"

But he was gone. I hung up, feeling totally frustrated. He had to be talking about me helping Frank and Dean, but why wouldn't he say it?

I picked up the phone and dialed.

"Bardini investigations," a girl's voice said.

"Is he there, Penny?" I asked. "It's Eddie."

"Hey, Eddie, how's it goin'? Yeah, he's here. Hold on."

She put me through to Danny.

"Lookin' for results already?" he asked. "You're a harsh taskmaster, buddy."

"I think I may have already gotten more results than I bargained for, Danny," I said. "I need to talk to you. I'm coming to your office. I can be there in about twenty minutes."

"Bring coffee," he said, and hung up.

# *Fourteen*

THE OFFICES OF Bardini Investigations were at 150 Fremont Street, between the Fremont Street Casino and Binion's Horseshoe Club, above a gift shop. When I opened the door Penny O'Grady looked up at me from her desk. I walked over and put a container down in front of her. She switched off her portable radio, cutting off the howling of what sounded like Buddy Holly. Dean Martin he ain't.

"Coffee or tea?" she asked.

"Tea," I said. "It doesn't take me long to learn."

"I've only been working for Danny for five years," she said. "It's taken me that long to get his files in shape, and for you to learn I drink tea."

Penny had come to Danny right out of college and convinced him to hire her. At the time he'd been running his office alone. Now she was twenty-seven and pushing him to make her a partner. She had freckles, long legs and red hair and the only thing that kept her from being a knockout was a snub nose she was saving to have fixed. In my opinion she was smart enough to be a partner, but Danny liked the idea of a one-man shop—with secretary. Neither of them had ever bothered to satisfy my curiosity about whether or not they were sleeping or had ever slept together.

"Go on in," she said. "He's not doing anything important."

"Thanks."

I went past her and through the door to Danny's office without knocking.

"What happened to you?" he asked, immediately.

"Does it show?"

"You're limping," he said, "and walking hunched over. And what happened to your head?"

I put my hand up to my scalp. I'd gotten past Penny, but not old eagle-eye Danny.

"I didn't think it showed."

"I'm a detective, remember?" he asked. "Speaking of which, I deduce that's coffee in your hand. Fork it over here."

I limped to his desk, sat across from him and handed him his coffee. He opened it, inhaled it, tasted it and then sat back and closed his eyes with a sigh. He liked it with four sugars, so I was always surprised his teeth didn't just drop out of his mouth.

"I swear I'm gonna fire that girl if she doesn't start makin' coffee." He opened his eyes and looked at me. "Okay, now give."

I told him the story, starting from when I entered my house without using the key and ending with Dori leaving the next morning.

"Not having to use your key to get in should have been your first clue," he commented when I was done.

"I came here so you could tell me something I don't know, Danny." My tone was a bit testy.

"Okay, okay," Danny said, "calm down. No damage to doors or windows, you said?"

"That's right."

"Then you were dealin' with pros," he said. "If you can describe them I can identify them for you."

"I got hit as soon as I walked in," I said. "I'm afraid I couldn't focus."

"Well," Danny said, "toss in the phone call you got this morning and it's obvious this is all because of this . . . Rat Pack thing you're involved in."

"Why didn't he just say so on the phone?"

"Maybe he thought your phone would be tapped."

"Why would someone tap my phone?"

"Maybe," Danny said, "he knows his own phone is tapped."

"You're saying he was with the mob?" I asked.

"Who else would have their phones tapped?"

"So that's why he didn't want to say Frank or Dean's name."

"Especially Sinatra's," Danny said. "And the guys they sent were real pro leg-breakers, not hit men, or you'd be dead."

"One of them told the other one to hold me so he could hurt me."

"Figures." Danny took time to sip his coffee and eye me over the rim. "There's nothing else you can tell me about them?"

"Well," I said, "they bitched at each other like an old married couple."

He laughed. "Why didn't you tell me that in the first place?"

"Why?"

"Because now I know who they are."

"Who?"

"Lenny Davis and Buzz Ravisi."

"Are they workin' for the mob?"

"They're pros," he said, "but not top of the line. They freelance as leg-breakers for the books, so I'm sure they've done some work for the mob at one time or another, but not for the big boys."

"So what's this mean for me?"

"It means that whoever's skin you've gotten under, he's not connected high up."

I thought about that for a moment.

"Or he doesn't want you to think he is."

"That's a big help."

"You want a gun?" he asked. "I can give you one, or get you one."

"What would I do with a gun?" I asked. "No, no gun." Not yet, anyway. Besides, I hadn't handled one since Korea. I'd shoot myself in the foot.

"This Dori," he said, then, "she the one with the big knockers from the Sahara?"

# Fifteen

BEFORE LEAVING DANNY'S OFFICE I verified for him that yes, Dori was the one with the big boobs from the Sahara, and he told me not to worry about Lenny and Buzz, that he'd check them out for me.

"I'm sure they did what they did just for the money," he said, "and nothing personal. If I pay them enough they might roll over on whoever they're working for."

"How much is enough?"

"I don't know," Danny said. "Don't worry, I'll handle it and let you know."

He hadn't picked up any word on the street about who might want to threaten Dean Martin, but he'd only been working on it since yesterday. I knew he had the word out, so I wasn't worried about that.

"You want to see a doctor?" he asked, before I left.

"I'm trying to be discreet, Danny."

"I got a guy who won't ask any questions," he said. He opened his drawer and gave me a card. "I'll call ahead and tell him you're comin'."

It wasn't a bad idea, so I said okay.

✳ ✳ ✳

"I don't see any cracked ribs on the X-ray," Doctor Gregory Edstrom said. He was holding my X-ray up to the light to show me. I didn't know what I was looking at, but I nodded.

"That's good."

"You've got a deep-tissue bruise on your back," he said, putting the X-ray down. "Take a few hot baths over the next few days, let the heat soak in. You got a heating pad?"

"I don't think so."

"Get one, use it, too."

"What about my knee?"

"No permanent damage there, but it's gonna hurt like a motherfucker for a while. Can you stay off of it?"

"Not likely."

His language belied his appearance, which was remarkably clean-cut and youthful, even though he had to be in his late forties.

"Here." He handed me a container of capsules. "Take these if the pain gets bad."

"What are they?"

"Demerol," he said. "They're strong, so don't take them unless you have to, and if you do, stay inside and don't drive." He tapped me on the shoulder. "Don't fuck up."

"Okay." I put them in my pocket with no intention of ever taking them out.

"Your scalp wound took only three stitches," he said. "I could put a bandage on, but if I don't your hairline will hide them and no one will notice."

"I don't need a bandage."

"Don't get it wet."

"Right."

"Your eyes are responsive, so you don't have a concussion. Far as I can tell you got away pretty cheaply from whatever you were doing."

"I was just—"

He held up his hand.

"I don't ask any questions, and I'd appreciate the same courtesy."

"Okay, fine. Are we done?"

"You're done," he said. "No running or jumping for a while. Keep your life down to a low roar."

"What do I owe you?"

"Fifty bucks."

I gave him cash.


I came away from Danny's doctor knowing pretty much what I'd known before, but fifty bucks poorer. Well, at least I had three stitches and some Demerol to show for it.

I was driving a '52 Caddy then, the car I'd bought to celebrate getting the job at the Sands. I loved that car, kept it in good shape, and was going to drive it as long as I could.

I got behind the wheel and rubbed my face with both hands. Did I have the balls to go to Jack Entratter, Frank Sinatra and Dean Martin and pull out of this thing? I'd only been at it a day and already I had a sore back, bruised ribs, swollen knee and stitches in my head—and it could've been a lot worse.

However, the longer I sat there fingering the bottle of painkillers in my pocket the angrier I got. Some sonofabitch had sent two leg-breakers to my house and then had the balls to call me the next day and play gangster games with me, thinking he could scare me off.

I was scared, all right, but just too mad to walk away.

# Sixteen

I DROVE BACK to the Sands and turned my Caddy over to a valet named Tim Daly.

"You ready to sell this car yet, Eddie?" Tim asked. "I'll make you a good price."

"No, not yet," I said. "Probably not ever."

"You always say that," Tim said, getting behind the wheel, "but everybody's got their price. Hell, this is Vegas, after all."

Well, he was right about that, anyway. It was Vegas: it was a place where too many people found their price.

I went inside, not sure what my next move was going to be—or what it should be. Tell Entratter what happened to me? Or Sinatra? Or Dean Martin? Or maybe just the little Ringmaster, Joey Bishop.

It turned out I didn't get to make the choice. As I entered the casino a large hand fell on my shoulder. I reacted violently, pulling away from it—or trying to—but it clamped down hard. I turned to throw a punch but he easily caught my fist with his other hand. All I got for my efforts was a twinge from my back and knee.

"Mack!" I said, recognizing him.

He released me and stepped back, eyeing me curiously.

"Damn it, what the hell—"

"I wasn't tryin' to hurt you."

"It's not you," I said, getting myself under control, "it's just—never mind. What do you want?"

"Somebody wants to talk to you."

"Who?"

"Come with me."

"Where?"

"The Flamingo."

The Flamingo. Bugsy's place—before Ben Siegel was shot in 1947. It was suspected that Bugsy's own people gunned him down because he had stopped being a team player and because expenses had skyrocketed. Bugsy had already cost them too much money. His place, however, remained in their hands, as did so many of the casinos on the strip.

"What's at the Flamingo, Mack?" I asked. "Or should I ask, who?"

"Come with me and find out."

I studied Mack Gray for a few moments while people walked around us. We were partly blocking the entrance while I made up my mind whether to go with him or not. In the end I figured, Why not? It kept me from having to decide my next move.

"All right," I said. "Lead the way."


"The way" led to a penthouse apartment at the top of the Flamingo. Not the best room the hotel had to offer, but pretty damn close.

Mack stopped in front of the door and knocked, then used a key to open it. I followed him in and looked around. It was about the size of Dean Martin's room at the Sands, but the furnishings were plush, all purples and red. It looked like the inside of a bordello. I had no doubt that Bugsy Siegel had approved the decor, and the rooms had been left the way he'd "designed" them even after his death.

"Who's room is this, Mack?" I asked.

"It's mine," a man's voice said.

I hadn't seen him when I walked in. He was standing at the window, which was a few steps up from the rest of the floor. His back was to me, his hands clasped behind him. He was a man of medium height and, from behind, all I could tell was that he was not young. He didn't have the bearing of a young man. I couldn't see the color of his hair, not with the light from the window distorting my view, but the one striking thing about him that stood out was his voice. It was a famous voice, and even with only a few words spoken I could tell before he turned around that I was in the room with George Raft.

Raft turned to looked at me, keeping his hands where they were. He was silver haired, in his sixties and had grown portly with the years, but he was still a dashing figure. To me he was still Gino Rinaldi from *Scarface.*

"Mr. Raft."

"Hello, Eddie." He took his hands from behind his back and slid them into his jacket pockets. "You mind if I call you Eddie?"

"Not at all."

"Mack," he said, "get Eddie a drink."

"Bourbon," I said, "rocks."

"I'll have one with my guest, Mack," Raft said.

"Yes, sir."

Mack moved to the bar at the far end of the room, as well-stocked as the one Dean had at the Sands.

Raft stepped down from where he stood and came across the room to me. I was surprised when he took one hand out of his pocket and extended it.

"Thanks for comin'."

I shook hands with him, and his grip was powerful. He was shorter than I was. In fact, I was surprised at how short he was, but then I was used to seeing him on the big screen.

Mack came over and handed each of us a drink, then stepped back, folding his arms across his chest.

"Sit down, Eddie," Raft said. "I wanna talk to you."

I sat on the plush sofa with my drink while he chose one of the armchairs across from me. He lit a cigarette with an expensive lighter after I turned down the offer of one.

"Where are you from, Eddie?"

"Brooklyn, New York."

"What part?"

"Red Hook."

"Tough boys from Red Hook."

"Some."

"I grew up in Hell's Kitchen, myself," he said. "Left there when I was thirteen. I fought and clawed my way to Hollywood—literally. I was a prizefighter for a while, you know."

"I know."

"You do?"

"I'm a big fan," I said. "You were a fighter and a dancer. When you got to Hollywood they wanted you to be a romantic lead, like Valentino."

He laughed, but I wasn't sure if it was because Hollywood had wanted him to be another Valentino, or because I knew that.

"Valentino," Raft said, shaking his head, "Me. That's rich."

"Pretty soon everybody realized you should be playing gangsters, especially after *Scarface.*"

"*Scarface,*" he said, and seemed to drift off into some kind of trance—maybe remembering when he was a huge star. He pretty much invented the whole gangster picture thing. "That was Muni's film. I prefer *They Drive by Night* or *Johnny Angel*, myself."

I looked at Mack, who was frowning at Raft. Apparently, this conversation was not going the way he had expected it to. I decided to say what I was thinking.

"Bogie, Cagney, Edward G, they wouldn't even have careers if it wasn't for you, Mr. Raft."

He focused on me, then.

"Naw," he said, waving my comment off with his hand, "those guys, they were great. They'll always be great. They're makin' a movie about me, did you know that?"

"I didn't know."

"Got some handsome young actor to play me. What's his name, Mack?"

"Ray Danton, Boss."

"Yeah, that's it," Raft said, "Ray Danton. You know who he is?"

"I've seen him in some things," I said. TV mostly. All the private-eye shows like '77 *Sunset Strip, Hawaiian Eye, The Untouchables, Bourbon Street Beat.* Okay, I'm a TV crime-show junkie when I'm home to watch it.

"How do you think he'll do?"

"Not bad," I said, "he won't do a bad job, but he's no George Raft."

Raft stood up, then, started pacing.

"I owned a piece of this place, you know," he said, "kicked in some bucks back when Benny needed it to open. Poor Benny . . ."

"Boss?" Mack said.

Raft turned, looked at Mack, then nodded and went back to his chair.

"Mack tells me Dean's got a problem that you're helpin' him with."

"You'd have to ask Dean about that, Mr. Raft," I said. "That's what I told Mack."

"I know, and Mack feels kind of hurt about bein' left out," Raft said. "Not that I blame him."

"No, sir."

"If you were to tell me what Dean's problem was," Raft offered, "maybe I could help."

"I'm sorry, Mr. Raft—"

"Just call me George, Eddie."

"Uh, George," I said, not at all comfortable with that, "I sort of promised Frank and Dean I'd keep my mouth shut. I wouldn't want to disappoint them."

"No," Raft said, thoughtfully, "wouldn't want to disappoint Frank. He gave me a part in *Ocean's Eleven,* you know. Small part. I play a casino owner. Lots of fun, this movie. Gonna be a hit."

"That's what I hear."

"Well," Raft said, "Mack will take you back down."

"I think Eddie can find his own way, Boss."

"Sure," I said, putting my glass down and standing up, "sure, I can find my way."

"I'm not gonna stand, if you don't mind," Raft said. "I'm . . . kinda tired."

"No, I don't mind at all, Mr. Raft."

"George," he said, "I told you, call me George. Us New York boys, we gotta stick together."

"Yes, we do."

I waited to see if he wanted to shake hands, and when he didn't make a move I walked to the door. When I turned around I saw Mack helping Raft up and walking him out of the room, probably to a bedroom to lie down.

I let myself out.

# Seventeen

I LEFT THE FLAMINGO and walked back toward the Sands. The marquee proclaimed it "A PLACE IN THE SUN." Underneath that it had the names of the Rat Pack members in descending order: Frank, Dean, Sammy, Peter Lawford and Joey Bishop. The day was living up to that name, the sun already baking the pavement beneath my feet.

When I got to the front doors of the Sands I stopped. I felt confused, didn't know what to do next. Finally, somebody from inside opened one of the doors, stepped out and held the door for me. That seemed to break the spell. I thanked him and walked in.

I looked around for Mack, not wanting to be surprised again, but I had left him at the Flamingo with Raft. My first instinct was to go for a drink, but my ribs were hurting and I had a pounding headache. I didn't want to take the powerful painkillers the doctor had given me, so I went in search of some aspirin. My feet, as if they had a mind of their own, took me to Jack Entratter's office. I figured since I was there looking for aspirin I might as well talk to him, fill him in, and maybe get some answers. Or maybe it was the other way around.

Jack's girl told him I was there and she buzzed me into his office.

"Could you get me some aspirin?" I asked, before going on.

"Of course, Mr. Gianelli," she said. "How many?"

"Uh, three should do it."

"And to take them with?"

"What?"

She smiled, blinked and said, "What would you like to drink, to take them with?"

"Just water."

"I'll bring them right in."

I thanked her and entered Jack's office.

"I know I told you to check in with me, kid," Jack said around his huge cigar, "but it ain't the end of the day, yet."

"I need to tell you some things," I said, "and ask you some things."

"Okay, siddown," Entratter said. "What's on your mind, Eddie?"

At that moment the girl opened the door and stepped in.

"What?" Jack barked.

"Mr. Gianelli's aspirin."

"Whataya need aspirin for?" he asked me.

"Pain."

"Okay, give it to 'im."

"Yes sir."

She handed me the pills and a glass of water, smiled and backed out.

"What's goin' on?" Entratter asked me. "Yer movin' funny."

I held up one finger, took the aspirin, washed them down and placed the glass on his desk. I then proceeded to tell him what had been waiting for me when I got home last night, and the call I got in the morning.

"Then," I finished, "when I got here Mack Gray grabs me and drags me over to the Flamingo to see George Raft."

Entratter frowned.

"I don't like the sound of this," he said. "What'd Mr. Raft want?"

"I'm not really sure," I said. "He wanted to know what I was doing for Frank and Dean."

"Did you tell 'im?"

"No."

"So what about the guys who kicked your ribs in?" he asked. "What'd you tell them? What'd they want?"

"I don't know," I said. "We never got around to exchanging words. They left me a message, though."

"What was it?"

"To mind my business."

He took the cigar out of his mouth and leaned forward.

"Who's business you been mindin', Eddie?"

"Frank Sinatra's," I said, "and Dean Martin's."

"Nobody else's?"

"No."

He replaced the cigar and sat back, thought for a moment before speaking again. He punctuated his words by pointing the cigar at me. I was glad it was the lit end and not the wet end. I was nauseated enough.

"You think the beating—"

"—and the call this morning."

"—were about what Frank asked you to do for Dino?"

"It can't be anything else, Jack."

He narrowed his eyes at me.

"You been *shtupping* anybody's wife, Eddie?"

"Why does everybody keep asking me that?" I demanded. "I don't make a habit of—no, no wives, Jack."

"Whataya want me to do, Eddie?" he asked. "Get ya out of this? Talk to Frank?"

"No," I said, "I don't want out, Jack. Not yet."

"Good boy."

"You ever heard of two lowlifes named Lenny Davis and Buzz Ravisi?"

I watched his face for his reaction and when he said, "Never heard of them." I believed him.

"They the guys you danced with?"

"Possibly," I said.

"You got their names pretty quick."

"That's why I got this job, ain't it, Jack?" I asked. " 'Cause I got the town wired?"

"What job?" he asked. "I thought this was a favor."

"Whatever it is," I said, "I'm still doing it."

"Good for you."

I took a moment to finish the water in the glass and set it back down.

"I'll be going, Jack," I said, "but there's one more thing."

"What's that?"

"Have you heard anything about Dean getting' somebody mad at him?" I asked. "Mr. Costello, Mr. Giancana, anybody like that?"

Entratter hesitated a long moment, then took the cigar out of his mouth. This time when he pointed it was the wet end.

"How would I know that, Eddie?" he asked, slowly.

"Well," I said, carefully, "Jack, I'd be a fool to think I was the only one who had the town wired. And not just this town. You worked in New York and Jersey. I just thought maybe you . . . heard something."

He took a moment to pluck some tobacco from his mouth with the thumb and index finger of his left hand while he maintained his hold on the wet thing with his right. It wasn't common knowledge that Jack Entratter represented the interests of Frank Costello in the Sands, but it was something Sands employees had all heard. In point of fact there were men with interests in the Sands living in New York, New Jersey, Miami, Boston, Chicago, New Orleans, St. Louis, L.A. and other places, and not all of them had Mafia ties. Some were just plain businessmen. Frank Costello, though, was a well-known Mafia figure in New York. To be blunt, he was the boss of the New York mob, and Jack was his man in Vegas.

"You sure these are the kind of questions you wanna be askin', Eddie?"

"If I'm going to do this favor right for Frank and Dino," I said, "yes, Jack."

"Well . . . I ain't heard anything like that, but if I do, I'll let ya know."

I smiled and said, "Frank and Dino and I would appreciate it, Jack."

"Yeah," Entratter said, "I know they will. Say, kid, you wanna gun?"

"What?"

"In case those two guys come back for ya," he said, opening a drawer in his desk. "I can give ya one now, or get ya somethin'—"

"Thanks, Jack," I said, "no gun. I'll be fine."

"Suit yerself," he said, closing the drawer. "I'll see ya later."

"See you, Jack."

Everybody was trying to give me a damn gun.

# Eighteen

IF JACK ENTRATTER SAID he hadn't heard anything about Dean Martin pissin' off some mob boss, or made guy, I probably should have taken his word for it. Jack worked for Costello, who might not be keeping him in the loop on some things. On the one hand, Frank was friends with Mo Mo Giancana and maybe he'd heard something. But on the other hand, he was friends with Dean, too. If Giancana wanted to take Dean out, why would he mention it to Frank?

But maybe I was jumping to conclusions. So far nobody had said anything about killing Dean. There were just these threats. It was probably too soon for me to arrange another meeting with Frank. What I should have been doing was trying to get a line on Davis and Ravisi. According to Danny the two were small-timers. If the Mafia wanted something done in Vegas they had a lot better ways to go before they decided to use two nothings like those guys.

I had Danny working on finding the two assholes who'd worked me over, but I had my own contacts, too. I wasn't a made guy or anything, but I knew some people who moved in those circles.

There was a guy named Lou Terazzo who came into the Sands to play blackjack all the time. He called himself "Lucky" Lou, but we all knew him as "Unlucky" Lou because the guy never won. Lou worked at the Riviera for Eddie Torres, who had taken over the operating duties of the Riv last year when the owner, Gun Greenbaum, was killed. It was pretty common knowledge that Torres was Meyer Lansky's man. So Lou may not have been much of a gambler, but he had big ears and he liked to brag to women about who he knew and what he knew. I needed to find out if Lou knew anything at all, or if it was all just talk for the ladies.

I went to the pits to see if Lou had been in today. His main game was blackjack although he was known to dabble in roulette and craps, too. But he hadn't been seen at any of those tables. Too early, I decided. He'd probably be in later, but I couldn't wait. I decided to go over to the Riv to see if I could find him and get him to talk to me.


The Riviera had been on the verge of receivership when Gus Greenbaum had been brought back to save it. A few years earlier Greenbaum had been the big boss at the Flamingo, but his health had gone bad and his wife, Bess, had made him quit. But then the boys wanted Gus back to save the Riviera, and they wouldn't take no for an answer.

Last year Greenbaum and his wife had gone to their retreat in Phoenix, Arizona, and there they'd been found one morning, in their bed, with their throats cut.

Word on the street had it that Gus had been killed for the same reason Bugsy Siegel had been killed, for being out of line. He'd wanted to sink two million bucks into an expansion of the Riviera, an expense the mob didn't need. His usefulness was at an end, and he ended up dead. Eddie Torres was a 30 percent owner of the Riv, and he'd been appointed its chief operating officer soon after Greenbaum's demise.

From what I knew the Riveria was now doing okay. As I stepped inside I could see that the place was jumping. The Riviera had more slot machines than any other casino on the strip, to go along with their table games and wheel of fortune. As well as lining the walls they had aisles of them bisecting their floor space. The slots were chrome and blue—the ones at the Sands were green—and in the square at the top where our slots said SANDS these said RIVIERA. If the slots were to become as popular as some said, I thought the casinos were going to have to get their own, rather than use the same models and simply put their names at the top.

I hadn't heard any complaints from anywhere about the way Ed Torres was running things at the Riv, certainly not from the people who were packing the place.

I checked out the lounge and didn't see Lou there, but I did see another face I knew, one of Unlucky Lou's coworkers, a guy named Mike "Bear" Borraco.

But Mike was nothing like a bear. As I approached him I was once again struck, as I always was, at how small his hands and feet were. Mike had as much to say about his job and his contacts as Lou Terazzo did, the only difference being I knew Mike was full of shit. Lou was a torpedo, a strong-arm man, maybe even a hit man for all I knew, but Mike, he was a gopher.

"Hey, Eddie G," Mike said as I reached him. "Whataya doin', checkin' out the competition?"

The bartender, whose ear Mike had been bending, gave me a grateful look and moved down the bar.

"I'm lookin' for Lou Terazzo, Mike," I said. "You seen him around today?"

"Lou? Yeah, I seen him." Mike used his palm to smooth down his hair, which would have worked if his hair wasn't so kinky. In his mind, though, he saw Elvis hair on his head. And since he looked a bit taller today than his usual five-four I was assuming he'd started wearing lifts in his shoes.

"But whataya need Lou for, Eddie?" he asked. "I can help ya with what you need."

Mike was looking at me like he was a puppy and I had a stick. He was just dying for someone to give him something meaningful to do.

"Do you know two guys named Davis and Ravisi?"

"Lenny and Buzz? Sure, I know 'em. They're freelancers. Bottom of the barrel, Mr. G," he said. "You'd do better with me, ya know?"

"I'm not looking to hire them, Mike," I said. "I'm looking to find out who sent them to my house to work with me over last night. Have they ever done any work for Mr. Torres?"

"Naw," Mike said, "Mr. Torres wouldn't hire them monkeys.

Why would he? He's got me and Lou and plenty of other good boys."

"Do you know where to find those two?"

Mike pulled on his lower lip while he thought. It wasn't a pretty sight. I could see that his bottom teeth were rotting away.

"Not off hand, but I'm sure I can find out."

I took out a fifty and handed it to him.

"There's another one when you give me an address," I promised.

"You got it, Mr. G," Mike said.

"Just call me Eddie, Mike."

"Can't," he said. "I'll get confused. Eddie's my boss."

"Okay, then call me Ed. Can you do that?"

"Sure, Ed," Mike said.

"I'd still like to talk to Lou, though," I told him, "so if you see him will you tell him I'm looking for him?"

"He owe the Sands money, Ed?" Mike asked.

"I can't answer that, Mike," I said. "That's between Lou and the Sands."

"He owes money to the Flamingo, the Dunes and the Sahara, too."

I already knew that, but I didn't let on to Mike that I did.

"Not my business," I said.

" 'Bout the only casino he don't owe is this one," Mike went on, "and that's only 'cause they won't let him gamble here."

"What about you, Mike?"

"Whataya mean?"

"You gamble?"

"Hell, no," he said. "I got better things ta do with my money then piss it away on cards or dice."

Like pissing it away on women, was my bet, but I kept that opinion to myself, too.

"Okay, thanks Mike."

"I'll get back ta ya as soon as I know somethin', Mr.—I mean, Ed."

"Thanks," I said. "I appreciate it."

I left the lounge and walked the remainder of the Riviera, still looking for Lou. I checked a couple of the restaurants, and even asked one of the pit bosses I knew if he'd seen him.

"Earlier today, yeah," the man said, "but not in the last couple of hours."

I thanked him and moved on. I figured I'd wasted enough time looking for Unlucky Lou. The chances were good he wouldn't be able to help me, anyway. And I really didn't expect to hear anything useful from Mike Borraco.

"Hey, Eddie?"

I turned and saw the pit boss running after me. His name was Steve Pepper, and he was a tall, good looking guy who I knew to be in his forties, even though he looked ten years younger.

"Yeah, Steve?"

"I just remembered," Pepper said. "Lou's been chasing after one of the girls in the show, her name's Carla. Maybe she can help you."

The Riviera's showgirls were the cream of the crop in town. I didn't think any of them would give a guy like Lou the time of day.

"Thanks, Steve," I said. "I'll check it out."

"Sure," he said, and went back to his pit.

I was torn between leaving the Riv or going to talk to the showgirl, Carla. I could see the front door from where I was, could envision myself going through it . . . and then what?

I turned around and headed for the theater.

# *Nineteen*

DORI ELLIS IS NOT the only showgirl I'd ever dated, but I'd been trying to cut down for a while. And it wasn't because they were long on looks and short on brains. That's a cliché. I've found showgirls who were pretty damn smart, with educations that came both from books and the street. No, they were simply driven by what they did, and had little time for anything else. Almost all of them I've known are either divorced or have been in and out of short-term relationships. Maybe that was why I asked Beverly to go with me to the Rat Pack show. Waitresses could be just as pretty and smart, but they certainly weren't career-driven—not yet, anyway.

When I went looking for Carla, the showgirl Pepper told me Unlucky Lou was seeing, I walked in on a full dress rehearsal and was reminded of why I started dating showgirls in the first place.

They were so damn beautiful.

I watched as the choreographer put them through their paces on stage. Legs flashed, breasts heaved, high heels made rat-a-tat sounds on the boards, blond-brunette-red hair flew, and they sweated—I mean, they perspired. There was nothing quite like a statuesque showgirl swea—perspiring.

As I watched I realized that I recognized one or two of them. That's the other thing about showgirls. Some of them are in it for the long haul, others come and went with the wind. While the core group was usually steady, there was a pretty good turnover rate, as well.

Big breasts were always good in my opinion, but for showgirls the most important thing seemed to be legs—long, long legs. Breast size varied, which made for a good variety, but when they were moving in perfect unison and those long legs were kicking and twirling, it was a sight to see.

Finally, rehearsal was over. I'd only had to stand and wait about fifteen minutes and then the girls started filing by me, heading for their dressing rooms. Some of them flirted in passing, others just threw me interested looks, while still others ignored me. The two I knew greeted me by name, but kept moving.

I also knew the woman who had been running the rehearsal. Her name was Verna and she had been a showgirl for a lot of years. Now she was in her forties, still striking, with red hair and the long, good legs. She came offstage dressed in a leotard, also glistening with perspiration.

"Hello, Eddie," she said. "What brings you here? Checking out my girls for your next conquest?"

"I wish, Verna."

"Or maybe you prefer them a little more . . . seasoned?" Verna was big-breasted, and since her retirement from full-time dancing she'd gained a few pounds which, from what I could see, had gone to all the right places. She wasn't built for dancing anymore, but she was perfect for, uh, other forms of recreation. A few extra lines around her eyes and a streak of gray in her red hair did nothing to alter her appeal to men.

"I'm actually looking for a particular girl, Verna," I said.

"What's her name?"

"Carla?"

"I got two Carla's, Eddie," she sad. "Which one?"

"Um, she's the one who's supposed to be seeing Lou Terazzo?"

Verna made a face.

"That's Carla DeLucca. Is she still seein' him? I warned her off, but they're young, they don't wanna listen to me. Shit, I've been through enough of those torpedoes in my day to know better, but do they listen?"

"I guess they have to make their own mistakes, Verna." I didn't want to add anymore fuel to her anger.

She heaved a sigh that was very interesting to me visually and which apparently cleansed her emotionally and said, "I guess you're right."

"Was she at this rehearsal?"

"Yes," she said. "A big brunette, too top-heavy for my taste—as a dancer, I mean—and her feet are too big. I don't think she'll be here past next year."

"But she's here now?"

"Yeah," Verna said. She gave me a leer. "You wanna go into the dressin' room and find her?"

"I'm tempted," I said, "but I'm afraid if I go in there I'm not going to want to come out."

She laughed, throwing her head back.

"If I let you go in there they may not let you come out," she said, placing her hand on my chest. "A handsome man like you . . . well, I'll go in and tell her you want to see her when she's dressed. You just wait out here where it's safe."

"Thanks, Verna."

She let her hand linger on my chest a little while longer.

"You and me have been in Vegas a long time, Eddie."

"Long time, Verna." She had been dancing at the Flamingo when I arrived in town.

"How come we never went out?"

I took her hand in mine, lifting it from my chest and holding it gently.

"You were always out of my league, Verna," I said, and then to try to lessen the sting added, "but then, you're out of everyone's league."

"Yeah," she said, sliding her hand from mine, "that must explain why this old broad is alone."

"Verna—"

"Shut up, Eddie," she said. "I'll go and tell Carla you're waitin' for her."

I guess that was another thing about the girls who were in it for the long haul. By the time they stopped dancing they were alone. Men in Vegas were looking for young girls, so someone like Verna would have to find a way to stay in the game—like becoming a choreographer. If not they'd end up waitressing or, worse, dancing in some club on the outskirts of Vegas, where tits and ass were more important than long legs and the ability to dance. Verna might have been a little bitter, but she was also one of the lucky ones.

# Twenty

I WAITED ABOUT A HALF an hour. During that time many of the girls had come out of the dressing room and either gone home or out to run their daily errands before returning later for the show. A couple of brunettes came out and when I asked if they were Carla they smiled politely and said no, Carla would be out soon. Finally, I got tired of waiting and approached the door to the dressing room. I knocked, opened it cautiously and said, "Hello? Anyone in here?"

"Come on in, handsome," a woman's voice said.

I entered and found myself face-to-face with a blond amazon. Even without the high heels she looked six feet. She was dressed for the street in blue jeans and a purple short-sleeved top that was being dangerously stretched by her breasts. In my opinion jeans were invented for dancers to wear. The denim clung tightly to their legs so you could see if a muscle even twitched. She had her long blond hair pulled back by a kerchief that matched her top.

"What can I do for you, lover?" she asked.

She had already applied her street makeup, which was considerably less than her stage makeup. Still, her lips were scarlet, and there was plenty of mascara surrounding her blue eyes.

"I'm, uh, looking for Carla De Lucca?"

"You mean I won't do?" she asked, putting her hands on her rounded hips.

"Oh, any other day I'd say yes without even hesitating," I answered.

"But not today."

"I'm sorry," I said. "You don't know how sorry."

"Well, don't be too sorry," she said. "There may be time after all."

"What do you mean?"

"Carla beat it out the back way about twenty minutes ago."

"Do you know why?"

"All I know is Verna came in and told her something, and she got dressed real quick and scrammed out the back. Is she runnin' from you? And if the answer's yes, why?" She eyed me with increased interest.

"I don't know," I said. "I guess I'll have to ask her when I see her. Which way did she leave?"

"Go out that door," she said, pointing to the other end of the dressing room, "and then there's a door that'll take you to the back parking lot."

"Okay, thanks."

"My name's Honey, by the way," she said. "Honey Sweet." She wrinkled her nose. "Stage name."

"Well, Honey, tell me, do you know Lou Terazzo?"

Now she wrinkled he nose in a totally different way.

"Do I? He's always hangin' around here, sniffin' after the girls."

"He's supposed to have a thing going with Carla," I said, "at least, that's the info I got."

"Well, that may be so, but it don't keep him from chasing the rest of us around here with his tongue hangin' out."

I decided to compliment her to see if she might have something else to tell me.

"Well, in your case," I said, "I guess you can't really blame him."

She liked that, and came closer. Her perfume was heavy, but it wasn't altogether unpleasant.

"You're sweet," she said.

"No," I said, "I thought you were, remember? Honey Sweet?"

She laughed and ran her hand up my arm. Her fingernails were painted the same scarlet as her lips.

"Well, maybe when you're done chasin' Carla you could come back."

"Maybe I could," I agreed. "When was the last time you saw Lou around here?"

"Earlier today."

"And you wouldn't happen to have an address for Carla, would you?"

"Actually, I do," she said. "I don't have much use for her, but her roommate and I are friends." She gave me an address of an apartment complex that was off the strip. "In fact," she added, "a few of the girls live there."

"Like you?" I asked, because it was expected of me.

"No," she said, "I have my own place somewhere a little more private. If you're lucky, maybe you'll see it some day."

"Hey," I said, "this is Vegas. It's all about luck. Thanks for talking to me, Honey."

"My pleasure, handsome," she said. "By the way, what's your name?"

"Eddie," I said, "Eddie Gianelli."

"Well, Eddie Gianelli," she said, "see you around."

"Yeah," I said, "see you."

Her perfume had started to get a little too heavy for me, and followed me outside like a cloud. Once I was in the Riviera parking lot, though, it dispelled and I was able to breath again. I took a few deep breaths, not only to get rid of the fragrance, but also the euphoria showgirls seemed to cause in men. It was something I certainly was not immune to, even after all these years in Vegas.

# Twenty-one

I WALKED BACK past Wilbur Clark's Desert Inn—Louie Prima and Keely Smith on the marquee—and collected the Caddy from behind the Sands. In the car I wondered if I wasn't going off on a tangent, somehow? Why was I chasing down Carla to find Lou when I didn't even know if Lou could help me? Was it because I couldn't think of anything else to do? And if that was the case what kind of real help could I be to Frank and Dean, who both apparently felt they could count on me?

Low-income housing had gone up all around the strip for the dancers and dealers and hotel employees, what I called the "non-rollers" of Vegas, who worked their asses off every day and never got to roll the dice, looking for their own luck. The complex where Carla and some of the other girls lived was just such a place. It was set up like a motel court, with a pool in the center that was designed to make you think you had a place to lounge and meet people.

As I entered the court I saw that the pool was so dirty nobody would be lounging there for a long time. The surface was covered with black and green areas of dirt and algae combining to form a condition most egghead professors try to create in beakers.

I wondered if Carla had even headed home when she ran out the back door of the Riv? Was she running or hiding from me, or from who she thought I might be?

Her apartment was on the second level so I climbed the stairs and started looking for her number. When I reached the door I saw that it was ajar. Maybe she had run back here, packed quickly and left so fast she didn't lock the door behind her. Still thinking this was all some misunderstanding, and that all I needed to do to straighten it out was talk to her, I went to the door and knocked.

"Hello? Carla? Anybody?"

I opened the door slowly and peered in. The place was in a shambles. For a moment I thought it had been burglars, but looking closer it resembled the scene of a fight. I'd seen some of the rooms in the Sands left this way after a fight had broken out between friends, usually fueled by the fact they were both losing.

I wondered if the police or sheriff had been called, but I didn't hear any sirens in the distance. The place had two bedrooms, a living-room area and a kitchenette. I stepped into the kitchen and saw that the fight—if that's what it had been—had not extended into there. It was not a place where anyone who cooked frequently lived. The tables and chairs were perfectly in place. On the counter was a cutting board with a variety of different-sized knives next to it. They were lined up by size, all neat and clean. None were missing.

I looked into both bedrooms. One was made up, the other a mess. However, the second room just looked lived-in to me, so apparently the fight—again, if that's what it had been—had been confined in the living room.

The sofa was askew, and the two armchairs had been overturned. The flimsy coffee table was in splinters, as was the single end table. I was no detective, but even I could see the grooves in the deep piled carpet where someone's heels had dug in while they were being dragged.

I went outside, looked back and forth and then, when I could put it off no longer, looked down. From this vantage point I could see there was a place where the dirt and algae in the pool had been disturbed, a place where someone might have gone into the pool. I continued to stare until I thought I could see a body at the bottom of the pool, but I was going to leave it to the police to find out for sure.

# Twenty-two

I WATCHED FROM THE BALCONY outside her room as two sheriff's deputies brought Carla DeLucca up from the bottom of the pool.

"Those guys are gonna have to be decontaminated," someone next to me said.

I turned my head and found myself looking at a tall, slender man in a lightweight gray sports jacket, gray slacks and a felt fedora.

"My name's Detective Hargrove," he said. "I'm with the Las Vegas P.D. And you are?"

"Gianelli," I said, "Ed Gianelli."

"And you're the one who called this in, Mr. Gianelli?" he asked.

"That's right."

I caught something on his breath, the unmistakable smell of Sen-Sen. He either thought he was going to meet some showgirls here, or like most cops he drank and was trying to cover the smell of booze. Since he was in his forties, with a busted blood vessel or two around his nose, I opted for the second.

He leaned his elbows on the railing right next to me and stared down at the pool.

"There's a job I wouldn't want to have."

"Shouldn't you be down there?"

"Naw," he said. "I'm pretty sure she's dead."

"Maybe," I said, "she fell."

"Nope," he said. "If she'd just fallen over the edge she would have hit the tiles. No, somebody picked her up and pitched her off. That's how she hit the pool."

"Wouldn't she have made a big splash?"

"Probably," he said.

"Somebody would have heard it, wouldn't they?"

"That's what we're gonna find out," Hargrove said. "We'll go around door to door, asking people what they heard. And do you know what they'll say?"

"What?"

"They didn't hear a thing, didn't see a thing."

Unfortunately I knew just what he was talking about. After all, I was from New York.

"So," he said, then, "tell me what you saw?"

Briefly, I told him about finding the door open and what I'd found inside.

"You didn't see her in the pool and then go inside?" he asked.

"No, sir," I said. "I didn't look into the pool until after I saw the inside of the apartment."

"And what made you look into the pool then, Mr. Gianelli?"

"I—I'm not sure," I said, truthfully. "To me the place looked like there'd been a fight. I came outside, leaned on the railing. I guess I was wondering what to do next when I looked down."

"Back up a moment, Mr. Gianelli," he said. "What do you mean, you 'were wondering what to do next?' Why wouldn't you just call the police?"

"I—I was trying to decide whether to go back inside and use the phone, or go to the office."

"And what did you decide, sir?"

"I went to the office," I said. "I told the desk clerk what happened and asked if I could use his phone."

"Did you know the deceased?" Hargrove asked.

"Never met her."

"Who lives here, Mr. Gianelli?" he asked.

"A girl named Carla DeLucca lives here with her roommate."

"And what's the roommate's name?"

"That I don't know."

He returned to face me, still leaning on the railing. Below me they were laying the body out on the tiles next to the pool.

"Why were you lookin' for her?"

I decided to tell the truth. There was no harm in it that I could see. The only thing I knew I wasn't going to mention to the police were the names Frank Sinatra and Dean Martin.

I explained how I'd gone to the Riviera looking for Lou Terazzo, and had been told by someone that Carla might know where he was.

"The Riviera," Hargrove said. "Buddy Hackett's playin' there, ain't he?"

I was about to say I didn't know when I realized he was right. I guess I had glanced at the marquee on my way into the Riv and now it sprang into my head with Buddy Hackett's name on it.

"Yes, I think he is."

"I love that guy," he said, "but you know who I really think is funny?"

I was afraid he was going to say me. Was he not believing what I was telling him. It was true, but that didn't mean he wasn't going to haul me in.

"Who?" I asked.

"Redd Foxx," he said. "That guy cracks me up. Is he in town, anywhere?"

"I don't know."

"Do you work for a casino, Mr. Gianelli?"

"Yes," I said, "I'm a pit boss at the Sands."

"The Sands," he said. "Frank Costello's got a piece of that place, hasn't he?"

"I don't know," I said. "I'm just a pit boss there."

"But you know Jack Entratter, right?"

"Of course," I said, "he's my boss."

"Yeah."

Maybe he'd wanted to see if I'd lie about knowing Jack.

"Lou Terazzo works for Eddie Torres," Hargrove said.

"You know Lou?"

"I know all the mob guys in Vegas, Mr. Gianelli," he said. "That surprise you, to hear that Lou's mobbed up?"

"Lieutenant—" I said.

"Detective," he said, "just detective."

"Detective Hargrove," I said, "I'm not naïve. I know the mob is in Vegas."

"That's an understatement, Mr. Gianelli," he said, cutting me off. "The mob is Vegas. You work in a casino, you work for the mob. That's just how it is."

Yeah, I wanted to say, and all the cops in Vegas are on the take.

Hargrove looked down towards the pool, nodded and waved to somebody.

"My partner is downstairs, Mr. Gianelli," he said. "He wants you to take a look at the body. Maybe you can identify it."

"I probably can't," I argued. "I never saw Carla DeLucca, I just heard about her."

"Well, maybe you'd be kind enough to take a look, anyway."

I was going to argue and ask why they didn't get the desk clerk to do it when I looked down. The girl was lying on her back, her show-girl's body looking curiously sunken. Her wet hair was plastered to her head, but even though it was wet I could see one thing clearly.

"That's not Carla DeLucca," I said. "I don't know who it is, but it's not her."

"You've gone from not knowing her to bein' able to I.D. her from up here?"

"I don't know her," I said, "but I know that she's a brunette, and that girl—" I pointed down, "—is definitely a blonde."

# Twenty-three

THEY ASKED ME a few more questions and then let me go. Hargrove's partner, a Negro detective named Smith, wanted to take me in, but Hargrove overruled him.

"He's a good citizen, Jake," he told his partner. "He called it in as soon as he found the girl. 'Course, he thought it was the wrong girl."

True, I had given Carla's name when I called. I didn't have any reason to think she wasn't the girl at the bottom of the pool, but then again I didn't have good reason to think she was. How was I supposed to know it was her roommate? In fact, it could have been anyone.

But the fact remained the dead girl was named Misty Rose—or Mary Reed, from some of the I.D. they found in the apartment. "Misty Rose" was her stage name, the name she danced under at the Riviera. I didn't know her; hell before today I had never heard of Carla DeLucca. I suggested that the detectives talk to Verna Ross at the Riviera. She was, I told them, the choreographer who also doubled as the girls' den mother.

So they let me go and I drove back to the Sands in a haze, wondering why Carla DeLucca had run out the back door rather than talk to me? And where was she now? Where was Lou? And how could this possibly have anything to do with what I was doing for Frank and Dean? The simplest answer was, it couldn't. . . .

Me finding a dead body was a coincidence, and not one that I ever wanted to repeat.

"A dead broad?" Jack Entratter repeated, staring at me from behind his desk? "Some little piece of trim who worked at the Riviera? Why you tellin' me about this, Eddie?"

"You told me to check in with you at the end of every day, Jack," I said. "This is what happened today."

"It ain't the end of the day, Eddie, and you been here twice already, today."

"It's after six, Jack," I argued. "That's the end of your work day."

He took his cigar out of his mouth.

"If you think my work day ever ends, kid, you're livin' in a dream."

"Believe me, Jack, I'm not livin' in a dream."

"Okay,' he said, "okay, so tell me, you think this dead broad's got anything to do with the threats bein' made to Dino?"

"No," I said, "it's got to be a total coincidence. I mean . . . I go looking for Lou Terazzo to ask if he knows anything about two guys who worked me over in my house because I was trying to do Dean Martin a favor. I end up looking for a girl named Carla DeLucca and finding her roommate, Misty Rose, at the bottom of a pool. Gotta be total coincidence, Jack."

"Then what are you worried about?"

"I don't like finding dead bodies, Jack."

"You ever found one before?"

"No, but—"

"Chalk this one up to experience, and keep workin' on the Dino thing."

I rubbed my face with both hands. He was right. I'd walked into something today that was none of my business. And I still had some work to do for Frank and Dean.

"What'd you tell the cops, Ed?" he asked.

"I told them the truth."

"You tell 'em why you were looking for Unlucky Lou Terazzo?"

"Well. . . . I told them he owed the casino money."

"That was good thinkin'."

I had had to lie about that because I hadn't wanted to bring any other names into it. The last thing Sinatra and Martin needed was the cops asking them about some girl they never heard of.

"Okay, kid?" Jack asked.

"Sure," I said, "sure."

I got up and headed for the door.

"You got my number in my suite," Entratter told me. "Use it if you have to."

"Okay, Jack."


I contemplated my next move over a drink in the Sands lounge. In a few hours Alan King would be cracking them up in there, but at the moment it was half empty and most of the people who were drinking there looked shell-shocked. It was a common look in Vegas. You saw it on the face of the woman who brought twenty dollars with her to gamble on the slots and lost it in the first machine she played. You saw it on the face of the guy who brought ten grand with him and he don't know what happened, but it's all gone the first day. What's she gonna tell her husband? What's he gonna tell his wife? Their problems are the same, just on different levels. And it was a toss up as to who was gonna be the maddest, her husband or his wife.

"Rough day, Eddie?"

Bev had come up next to me and startled me.

"Yeah," I said, "the roughest. I found a dead girl today."

"What?" She put her hand on my arm. "Oh, Eddie, I'm so sorry. That must have been terrible for you. Was she, uh, a friend of yours?"

"No," I said, "I didn't even know her. I just . . . stumbled onto the body."

"Still, it must have been a shock."

"And then the cops questioned me, almost like I was a suspect."

"Why would they do that?"

"They're cops," I said, "it's their job."

She ordered some drinks from the bartender and put her tray on the bar so he could weight it down.

"Gee, I'm sorry you had such a bad day, Eddie."

"Ah," I said, "I'm sorry I dumped it on you, Bev."

"That's okay," she said.

She picked up the heavy tray with grace and surprising strength. I thought I would have staggered under the weight.

"If you want to talk later, Eddie," she said, "I'm a real good listener. Just give me a call."

"I might do that, Bev," I said, "I might just do that."

# Twenty-four

FOR VEGAS anytime was the shank of the evening. If I'd been on the clock I would have been in my pit, trying to keep high rollers happy while at the same time trying to keep the casino from losing too much money. It's a delicate balancing act, and I believed that one day it would be two very specific jobs in Vegas casinos. Let the pit guy concentrate on the game, and let someone else keep the gambler happy.

I decided to go and take a look at my pit and see what was going on. The blackjack tables were full, with only an occasional empty seat. A couple of my big-money guys were there, which meant their wives would be on a slot machine somewhere.

Pete Dawson played a hundred dollars a hand minimum, often bumped it up to five hundred. But there was never any rhyme or reason that I could see when he would bump up the bet. It seemed to take place on a whim. It used to drive me crazy until I found his wife at a slot one day and decided to ask her about it. . . .

Her name was Lisa Dawson, and she had probably been a heckuva looker twenty, maybe ten years ago. These days she was a blowsy forty-five or so, her once taut figure now full, almost sloppy. She had large breasts and dressed to show them off. Her black hair came out of a bottle, and her once pretty face was mottled from drinking and heavy with pancake make-up to hide it. And yet there was a sexy, slutty quality to her. More than once she'd offered to take me to a room while her husband played blackjack, but I always declined.

The day in question was no different. I had been relieved in the pit and in passing a bank of slot machines had seen her there. I detoured and walked over to her.

"Hello, Lisa."

She looked up from her machine, annoyed that someone would interrupt her, but when she saw it was me she smiled widely.

"Eddie G," she said. "Come to take me up on my offer to let me fuck your brains out while my husband loses all our money?"

"He never loses it all, Lisa," I said, "and if I did let you fuck my brains out it would probably ruin me for other women."

"Well, you're right about that," she said, with a wicked smile. She turned to face me, giving me a clear view of her plunging neckline. I had to admit her breasts looked inviting, and that shadowy cleavage was intriguing. The gold lamé dress she wore clung to her lovingly, but I was sure she was firmly corseted into it. I didn't want to be in the same room with her when she got undressed and removed it. Suddenly, the air of intrigue was gone.

"I just wanted to ask you a question about your husband."

"Oh," she said, "him."

"I'm wondering about his strategy."

"Strategy?" she asked. "What strategy?"

"Well, he bets a hundred or two hundred most of the time, but every so often he jumps the bet up to five hundred. I was wondering if there was a strategy behind it?"

She studied me for a moment, then dropped a coin in the slot machine and pulled the handle. The reels went around, flashing red, yellow and orange, and then stopped with a lemon between two cherries.

"If I tell you," she asked, "would it help you beat him?"

"Well, no—maybe, but—"

"Just say yes," she said. "I'd love to see him lose for once."

She was right. Even though I couldn't see a strategy to his play, he seemed to win all the time.

"Okay," I said, "it would help."

She looked around, then crooked her finger at me and leaned forward.

"He bets five hundred every time a pretty girl comes to the table or walks by."

"What?"

"It's true," she said. "Any time a pretty young girl is around he tries to impress her by betting five hundred dollars."

I stood straight up.

"That's it? That's his strategy?"

"That's it," she said. "Can you use that?"

"I don't think so," I said. "If that's all it is then it's a matter of luck."

"Can't your dealer do something when they see a pretty girl? Deal from the bottom?"

"Sorry, Lisa," I said. "That would be cheating."

"Oh," she said, "and the casinos don't cheat, right?"

"Not while I'm in the pit," I told her, and walked away. . . .


I watched Pete play a few hands and saw that he'd stopped betting five hundred, even when a pretty girl passed. I looked around for Lisa but she wasn't anywhere to be found. Maybe she'd stopped coming with him to the casino. Not that I minded.

I nodded to Tom Huston, who was manning my pit in my stead, and moved on. I made a slow circuit of the casino floor, comparing it in my mind to the Riviera. All-in-all I preferred the ambience of the Sands to those of the Riv, the Sahara and some of the other properties. We didn't have as many slots, since Entratter was on the same wavelength as me and didn't think the one-armed bandits were going to become as popular as other people in the business were saying. Or maybe I was just more comfortable there after so many years. It was, after all, my home.

I stepped outside. The heat had relented a bit, but we were still in the middle of the desert. The temperature didn't drop significantly until after the sun actually went down.

I'd had a full day already, running around after Lou Terazzo and Carla, finding a dead body. I was tired. I decided to go home, maybe stop someplace for a bite to eat. Danny might have found something out during the day, or even Mike Borraco. One of them might call me and I thought I should be home if they did.

# Twenty-five

I WATCHED MY REAR-VIEW mirror all the way home. I didn't
know if Ravisi and Davis had followed me home last night or had
been waiting for me there, but I didn't want to take any chances. Not
that I knew what I was doing. Several times I thought I spotted a car
following me, only to have it turn and disappear. When I got home I
pulled into the driveway of my little house, then waited a few moments before I got out. When I got to my front door I fitted the key
into the lock and opened it very carefully. When nobody grabbed me
and pulled me inside I stepped through the doorway, then closed and
locked the door behind me.

My house is small, and all on one level. It didn't take me long to go
through it and determine that I was alone. When I was reasonably sure
I was safe I went to the kitchen, scraped the Chinese I'd brought home
with me onto a plate, got myself a beer and sat down to eat. I went
over the day again in my head and decided that if I was going to do
Dean Martin any good I had to forget about finding the body of Misty
Rose. Like Jack Entratter had said, I had to chalk it up to experience.

However, the fact remained that somebody out there didn't want
me helping Dino, and they had sent two gorillas to make their point.
It seemed logical to me—not being a detective, and all—that whoever
sent them was behind the threats. And I had two names, which

Danny Bardini and Mike Borraco also had. I decided to let those two keep their ears to the ground and wait for them to get back to me. Going out on my own to find some other contacts had not turned out so well today.

But there was nothing I could do about my curiosity. Why had Carla DeLucca run away when she heard I wanted to talk to her? What I had to find out from Verna was what she'd said to Carla. Had she told her, "There's a man outside to see you," or had she said my name? If she'd told Carla my name, then the woman had run from me and that was something I didn't understand.

Women didn't always swoon over me, but they didn't usually run from me, either.

I finished what was in my plate, left the rest in the boxes and put those in the refrigerator. I pulled out one more beer and took it into the living room with me to catch the news.

They covered the discovery of Misty Rose's body, but kept my name out of it. I learned that Misty not only danced at the Riv, she stripped at one of the local clubs, as well. Police suspected that some amorous Romeo had followed her home from work, pushed his way into her apartment, and ended up killing her. They didn't say whether or not she'd been dead when she went into the water.

More curiosity on my part, or maybe just an inability to believe in coincidence. Did Misty's murder have nothing to do with Carla running from me? Was Misty dead when Carla heard I wanted to talk to her? Did Carla think I was a cop or, worse yet, the killer? And where was Unlucky Lou Terazzo? What was his part in all this? Could he have been the amorous Romeo?

By the time I refocused on the TV a movie had started. I was about to turn it off when I realized it was an old John Wayne western. I decided to go ahead and watch it, but I hadn't gotten a half hour into it when my eyes began to droop, and then I dropped off to sleep. I didn't know I was asleep, though, until someone pounding on my door woke me up.

I leaped to my feet, eyes wide, in a cold sweat, and stood there wondering what was going on. The move did nothing for the pain in my side which, amazingly, had left me alone for most of the day. Now it was back, though, and so was the headache.

When I realized someone was knocking I looked around for a weapon. I had to choose between the beer bottle and a lamp. I decided on the bottle, reversed it so I could hold it by its long neck and went to the door.

When I peered out the small eye level window in my door I saw Detective Hargrove standing on my doorstep with his partner.

I opened the door and looked at them through the screen door.

"Detective Hargrove," I said. "What brings you here at—"

"Midnight," he said, cutting off my question. "Don't tell me a casino bigwig like you hits the sack at midnight, Mr. Gianelli."

"Fell asleep in front of the TV."

"Did ya watch the news to see if they'd mention your name?" the other detective asked. I'd forgotten his name. "Guess you were disappointed, huh?"

"No," I said, "as a matter of fact, I wasn't. I was glad not to hear my name. You guys want to tell me why you're here?"

"We'd love to," Hargrove said. Apparently, he thought that was an invitation to enter. He opened the screen door and stepped through. I had no choice but to back off or let him walk into me. His partner followed and closed the door behind them.

"Where'd you go today, Gianelli?" Hargrove asked.

I noticed he wasn't calling me "Mister" anymore. I'd seen enough old movies to know that wasn't a good sign.

"When?"

"After you left us this afternoon," Hargrove said. "Account for your movements."

"Why?"

"Humor us," his partner said. I suddenly remembered his name was Smith, and then felt stupid for forgetting it.

I thought about resisting, then figured, what the hell? I wasn't guilty of anything.

I told them I went back to the casino to check in with my boss and get my work done.

"And you were there the whole time?"

"Yes."

"Can anybody vouch for that?"

"My boss."

"Jack Entratter?" Hargrove asked.

"That's right."

"Yeah, he's a reliable witness."

"Some of the other employees saw me."

"Don't lie to us, Gianelli," Smith said. "If we go down there and ask around and find out you lied—"

"I'm not lying." Actually, I wasn't, but I wasn't telling the whole truth, either. I was still leaving the Rat Pack out of all my explanations. But I had gone back to the Sands, and I had gone home from there. "Go ahead and ask them."

"Oh, we will," Smith said. He turned and headed for the door.

I looked at Hargrove. "Can you tell me what this is about?"

He considered it for a moment, almost followed his partner, then turned back with a kind of "what-the-hell" shrug.

"The other girl," Hardgrove said, "the one you were lookin' for?"

"Carla DeLucca?"

"We found her in a Dumpster out behind the Riviera."

"Dead?"

"Mr. Gianelli," he said, "we don't often find live girls in Dumpsters."

# Twenty-six

IT WAS THE END of a long day that had resulted in the death of two women I didn't know. Still, I was obviously a suspect in their deaths, otherwise I would not have received that late-evening visit at my home from Detectives Hargrove and Smith.

Since agreeing to try to help Dean Martin I had been beaten up in my home, found a dead woman, and become a suspect in two murders. I had every reason to pull out and tell both Dean and Frank thanks but no thanks, I didn't think I could help them. But there was still my curiosity to be appeased, and the only way to do that was to find Unlucky Lou.

I was trying to decide between another beer and bed when the phone rang. I checked the clock. Two A.M.

"Mr. G, that you?" I recognized the voice right away. Mike Borraco. I had given him my home number as well as my number at the Sands.

"Mike?"

"Hey, it is you," Mike said. "I hope I ain't callin' too late."

"This is Vegas, Mike," I said. "It's never too late." I didn't want him to know I was on the verge of turning in for the night. "What can I do for you?"

"I think I might have a location on Unlucky Lou," Mike said, "but I won't know for sure until tomorrow. Will I be able to reach you?"

"You can call me at the Sands and leave a message," I said. "I'll probably be out and about."

"Okay," Mike said. "Hey, I heard about Carla and her roommate. Tough break. You think Lou had anything to do with that?"

"I don't know, Mike."

"Whatever you was lookin' for him about musta been important, huh? Somebody's out there killin' people over it. I was thinkin'. . . ."

"Thinking what, Mike?"

"Well . . . I was thinkin' the info about Lou might be worth a little more money than what we discussed."

"Mike," I said, "I have no idea why those two women were killed. It's got nothing to do with why I was lookin' for Lou, believe me."

"Just a coincidence, huh?"

"Exactly," I said. "Just a coincidence."

"Uh-huh. Well, I'll call ya tomorrow, Mr. G."

I didn't know where the "Mr. G" stuff came from, but I said sure and hung up. I had the feeling Mike didn't know anything yet, and was just trying to jack up the price.

I hung up and decided to go to bed. I was tired, and sore, but that wasn't the reason. I just wanted the day to end. Maybe after a good night's sleep I'd decide to hell with the whole thing and go back to my pit.

I woke up the next morning to a pounding on my front door. Thinking it was the police again I wasn't in a hurry to answer it. Wearing only pajama bottoms I stumbled to the door and opened it. Standing there was Frank Sinatra. He was wearing a white tuxedo, no tie, his shirt collar open. At the curb was a black limousine with the motor running. The back window was rolled down about halfway and I thought I could see a woman's head, blonde.

"Frank."

" 'Mornin', pally," he said. "Got any coffee?"

"I, uh, can put some on," I replied. "What time is it?"

"I'm not sure. Eight? Nine?"

"Come on in." I backed away from the doorway. "What about your . . . friends?"

I thought I heard giggling from the car and revised my estimate. He had at least two women in there.

"They're fine," he said, waving a hand negligently. "They've got champagne, and Henry's with them." I assumed he meant Henry Silva. "I need coffee."

"Yeah, sure. I, uh, lemme get some pants on. Have a seat."

I left Frank Sinatra in my living room. I pulled on a pair of slacks and a T-shirt, ran a comb through my hair and hurried back out. He wasn't there, but I heard something clinking in the kitchen.

As I entered I found him with a can of coffee on the counter, using an opener on it.

"I can do that, Frank."

"I got it, Eddie," he said. "Have a seat. Want some toast? Got any bread?"

"Second drawer." I was thinking, Frank Sinatra is making me breakfast! And then I tried to get past that.

He'd obviously been up all night, had probably gone out directly from the Rat Pack show in the Copa Room. But his eyes seemed bright and clear, his hair was perfectly combed. Even though his jacket was wrinkled and his tie was missing, he still looked like he was ready to go on, or to shoot a movie.

"Aren't you supposed to be on a set somewhere?" I asked. *"Ocean's Eleven?"*

"They'll wait." The hand wave, again. He spooned out the coffee, put the lid on and set it on a burner. "They can't do a thing without us and then we always get it in one take. Know what Smokey calls us? 'One-Take Charlies.' Stove works, I hope."

"It works." My kitchen was filthy. "Cleaning lady hasn't been in."

"Forget it," he said, coming over to sit across from me. "You should see some of the dives I've had coffee in."

"Frank . . . you weren't just passin' by."

"You're right," he said, reaching across the table and tapping me on the arm. "I got your address from Jack before I left the Sands last night. I wanted to talk to you."

"About what?" I asked. "I've only been on this thing for a day and—"

"Jack told me what's been going on. A dead showgirl? What's that all about?"

"I don't know," I said, "and it's two dead showgirls."

"Two?" Sinatra looked shocked. "What kinda nut kills two gorgeous babes?"

I shrugged helplessly.

"You know, Ed," Sinatra said, "if you want to pull out you can."

"Frank, I don't think the two girls have anything to do with you or Dean. That's just somethin' I kinda walked into."

"You did have two clydes work you over, though, right?" Frank asked. "Warn you away from Dean?"

"Yeah," I said.

"They hurt you bad?"

"A bump on the head, a few sore ribs," I said.

Frank smiled. "You and me, we got worse than that when we were kids, right?"

"Right, Frank," I said, without much enthusiasm.

"Hoboken, Brooklyn, not much difference between the two."

I didn't agree with that. No Brooklyn boy would ever agree that any part of New Jersey was the same as Brooklyn, but I kept that opinion to myself.

The room began to fill with the smell of percolating coffee. Sinatra sat back in his chair and appeared to breath the aroma in deeply. I seemed to remember that he had recorded something called "The Coffee Song," a few years back.

"So you're still with us, then?" he asked.

"I'm with you, Frank."

"Any word yet? Any . . . clues?"

"None. I talked to everyone at the hotel. Nobody remembers envelopes being delivered for Dean. Has he been at the set?"

"He was there yesterday, and he'll be there today." He shot his cuff and looked at his watch. "I've got just enough time for a cup."

He stood up, found where I kept the cups and poured us each full. We both sipped and made the same face.

"I make a lousy cuppa joe," he said, and pushed his away.

To me coffee's coffee, so I continued to drink it.

"Walk me to the door."

He stood up and I followed. We walked to the door shoulder to shoulder.

"I've got somethin' for you."

"What?"

"It'll be here in a couple of hours. When do you go to work?"

"I'm off the clock."

"Good," he said, "then you'll still be here when it arrives."

He opened my front door and stepped outside. We stood in the doorway and shook hands. I heard the girls laughing in the car. They didn't seem to be missing Frank at all.

"Can you give me a hint?" I asked.

"I don't want to ruin the surprise." He started down the walk toward the limo, then turned nimbly. "You need any money? For expenses or something?"

"No," I said, "I'm good, Frank."

"Okay."

"Hey, Frank."

He turned and looked at me expectantly. I looked around, saw no one, but stepped outside anyway, to get closer to him so I could lower my voice.

"Frank, do you think anyone . . . well, connected, is after Dean?"

"Kid," he said, though he wasn't that much older than me, "if anyone 'connected' was after Dean, he'd be dead by now. *Capice?*"

# Twenty-seven

I DIDN'T MEAN TO WAIT for Frank Sinatra's gift to arrive, but as it turned out it took me that long to get myself around. When the knock came at the door I decided that entirely too many people knew where I lived.

When I opened the door a big guy was standing there blocking out the sun. He was even bigger than Mack Gray.

"Oh, no, not again." I figured I was in for another beating.

"Huh?" he said.

"Can I help you?" I asked.

"You Gianelli?"

"That's right."

"Eddie Gianelli, right? Eddie G?"

"That's me."

"Then I got the right place."

"The right place for what?"

"Frank sent me."

"Frank . . . Sinatra?"

"That's right," the man said. "He told me to tell you I was your gift? You know what that means?"

"Yeah," I said, "yeah, I'm afraid I do."

∗   ∗   ∗

His name was Gerald Epstein but he told me I could call him Jerry. I didn't want to call him anything, because I didn't want him around.

He was sitting at my kitchen table, drinking coffee Frank Sinatra had made, while I tried to convince him he didn't have to stay.

"I don't leave until you do."

"You mean . . . you're goin' with me everywhere I go?"

He nodded.

"Until Frank tells me not to."

"Jerry . . . are you carryin' a gun?"

"Of course," he said, looking at me as if I was nuts. "What kinda bodyguard would I be if I didn't have a gun?" He pulled aside his jacket to show me the piece in his shoulder holster. I recognized it as a .45, same thing I carried in the army.

"Jerry, if you get caught with that—"

"I got a permit."

That figured.

"Did Frank tell you what's goin' on?" I asked.

"He said a coupla guys worked you over. He said I should make sure that does not happen again."

"Did he tell you who worked me over? Or why?"

"No," he said, "but I don't have to know that to do my job."

"Well, let me ask you," I said, "do you know two guys named Lenny Davis and Buzz Ravisi?"

"No. Are they local?"

"I think so."

"I ain't local," he said. "I'm in from New York."

"When did you get here?"

"Last night."

I hesitated to ask the next question. Partly because I didn't want to know the answer, partly because I thought I already knew.

"Who do you work for in New York, Jerry?"

"I work for Mr. Giancana. And while I'm in Vegas, I work for Frank."

That's what I was afraid he was going to say. I'd spent my life trying to stay out of street gangs when I was growing up, and away from the mob as an adult. I'd thought I could work in the casinos in Vegas and stay away from them, and I thought I had done pretty well for twelve years—except maybe for Jack Entratter—but now . . .

. . . Frank Sinatra . . .

. . . Sam Giancana . . .

. . . I guess the connection was unavoidable.

# Twenty-eight

I CALLED DANNY BARDINI and he agreed to meet me for breakfast at the Horseshoe, Benny Binion's place on Fremont Street. Benny had arrived in Vegas the same month Bugsy Seigel opened the Flamingo. He'd left a violent past behind in Texas, where he had a reputation as a gambling king and a killer. They say he arrived with two million dollars in a suitcase. Four months later he bought the old Eldorado Club, changed the name to the Horseshoe Club and turned it into one of the most popular casinos in Las Vegas.

Danny was waiting at a booth in the back of the Horseshoe's coffee shop.

"Who's he?" Jerry asked, as we entered.

"A friend of mine."

"A cop?"

"No," I said, "he's not a cop. He's a P.I."

Jerry made a face.

"Same difference."

"Jerry, why don't you sit at the counter and have what you want."

"You buyin'?" he asked.

"Yeah, I'm buyin'."

He looked over at the counter, and then at the booth Danny was sitting in.

"Don't worry," I said. "You can see me from there."

"Okay."

As he settled onto a stool—almost two stools—I walked over to where Danny was waiting.

"Who's the giant?"

"That's Jerry," I said, sliding in across from him. "He's a gift from Frank Sinatra."

"Frank never heard of jewelry?" Danny asked. "Or cars? You know, I heard that Elvis Presley gives everybody cars, even people he doesn't know. Why don't you work for Elvis Presley?"

"Give Elvis my number," I said. "If he calls I'll work for him. Meantime, what did you find out?'

"Can we order, first?"

"Sure."

As I looked at the menu a waitress came over.

"You Eddie G?" she asked.

I looked up at her. A waitress in the Horseshoe's coffee shop and she looked like she should be a showgirl—but considering how many showgirls had shown up dead lately, maybe she was better off where she was.

"That's right."

"Um, the big man at the counter? He says you're payin' for his breakfast?"

"He's right."

"Mister," she said, "he ordered two dozen pancakes."

I turned and looked at Jerry, who was staring into a mug of coffee. As if he felt my eyes on him he turned his head and looked over, his face expressionless.

"So give him his pancakes," I said.

She shrugged and said, "Okay." She turned and nodded to the man behind the counter, then looked at us. "You boys ready to order?"

"Yeah," Danny said. "Pancakes sound good but I'll just have a stack."

I ordered scrambled eggs, bacon, home fries, toast, juice and coffee.

"Two dozen pancakes," Danny said as she walked away. "This I gotta see."

"Danny," I said, "tell me you found somethin' for me, because I'd hate to have to rely on Mike Borraco."

"That weasel?" he asked. "He's scammin' you, Eddie, if he says he can get you somethin'."

"Probably," I said. "I just have him looking for Unlucky Lou Terazzo."

"You and the cops," Danny said. "What did you get yourself into, pal?"

"The cops talked to you?"

Danny nodded.

"A dick named Sam Hargrove. I know him, and he knows we're friends."

"What'd he ask you?"

"Wanted to know if you were violent," Danny said. "Have you ever beat up any women? Did you have somethin' against showgirls."

"What'd you tell him?"

" 'No, no and no,' " he quoted. "Those words, exactly. So what'd you walk into, bub?"

"Danny, I don't know. I went lookin' for Lou Terazzo just to see if he might know somethin' about the two goons who worked me over."

"Why Lou?"

I shrugged. "I just figured they were members of the same fraternity, you know?"

"And?"

"And I never found him. Instead, I get put onto a showgirl named Carla and while I'm lookin' for her I find her dead roommate."

"And now she's dead, too."

"That's what Hargrove and his partner told me last night."

"What does this have to do with Dean Martin?"

"Fuck if I know," I said. "Nothin', probably."

"You mean this is all a coincidence?"

"It's got to be."

He sat back in his chair and stared at me.

"What?"

"I hate coincidences, Eddie. You know how I hate coincidences."

"What else could it be?" I asked. "I just happen to go looking for Lou Terazzo, and he's involved with the threats on Dean Martin? Isn't that a coincidence, too?"

"Those two girls got killed for some reason."

"That's got nothin' to do with me or the Rat Pack," I insisted.

"So you're still lookin' into this for Sinatra and Dino?"

"I gave my word."

I'd given a lot of thought to quittin', but the truth was I didn't want either Sinatra or Dino to think badly of me, or even Entratter. It might have been an ego thing, but there it was. I couldn't quit.

The waitress came with our breakfast and set it all down. Danny was lookin' past me, so I turned and saw that Jerry had started in on his two dozen pancakes.

"Maybe he needs a shovel," Danny said to the waitress.

She laughed and walked away.

"Danny . . ."

He dumped some butter and syrup on his cakes and said, "I've got nothin' on Ravisi or Davis, Eddie. They've disappeared."

"What about who they were workin' for?"

"They'll work for anybody who can run two dollars together."

"What about big boys like Costello or Giancana?"

"Why would they give work to bums like that," Danny said, "when they've got Man Mountain Jerry, over there? By the way, what's his last name?"

"Epstein."

"A Jew? Maybe he works for Lansky?"

"He says he's from New York, where he works for Giancana. Now he works for Frank."

"Mo Mo sent Frank one of his boys? Guess they're as close as everybody says, huh?"

"I don't care," I said. "Frank can be friends with anybody he wants."

"They say the mob got him *From Here to Eternity.*"

"What's the difference?" I asked. "He made the most of it, didn't he? Got his career back on track?"

Danny shrugged around a mouthful of pancakes. He had a

smudge of syrup on one corner of his mouth. I piled some eggs and bacon onto a piece of toast and shoved it into my mouth.

"If they bought him the movie, they coulda bought him the Oscar, too."

"Maybe," I said, "but they can't sing for him. He does that on his own."

"I hear he's pushin' for Kennedy," Danny said. "That's some triangle, huh? Frank, Mo Mo and JFK?"

"We're gettin' off the subject, Danny."

"Okay, okay," Danny said. "I'll keep lookin' for these guys. I don't think we're gonna find out who they're workin' for until we actually meet them face to face."

"What if they're in a hole in the desert somewhere?" I asked.

"You better hope they ain't," he said, licking the syrup off his lip. "They sound like your only lead."

# Twenty-nine

AFTER BREAKFAST I FOUND OUT that Jerry had washed down his pancakes with two pots of coffee and a quart of orange juice. He'd also had a half a dozen pieces of toast.

"I've never seen a breakfast check come to that much," Danny said, when the waitress brought the check over. "That looks more like dinner at the Ambassador Room."

"Luckily, I've got a tab here," I said, signing my name on the check.

"Entratter got you a tab here?"

"And other places," I said. "I can pretty much eat at most of the places in town."

"And you eat in coffee shops?"

"Most of the time."

"Damn," Danny said, "I've got to get you to take me someplace more expensive."

"You find those two guys for me and I'll take you anywhere you want to go."

"You're on."

✳ ✳ ✳

Walking out onto Fremont Street I asked Jerry, "You get enough to eat?"

"Yeah," he said. "I'm full. The pancakes is very good there."

"Yeah," I said, "it's one of the best coffee shops in town."

"The best coffee shops in the world are in New York," he said.

"You think so?"

"I know so."

"You get pancakes this good in New York?" I asked.

"On every corner."

"Yeah," I said, "that's pretty much the way I remember it."

"You from New York?"

"Brooklyn," I said. "I grew up in Red Hook."

"The Hook was tough," he said, "but I grew up in Bed-Stuy."

Bedford-Stuyvesant was one of the toughest neighborhoods in Brooklyn, but I would put my childhood in Red Hook up against his any day.

"You ain't got no accent," he insisted.

"I've been away from there a long time."

"I hate leavin' New York," Jerry said. "And I hate this town."

"What've you got against Vegas?"

"It ain't got no heart."

"It's got a pulse," I said.

"It's all lights and cheap gamblers," he said. "And the broads is phony. I can't wait to go back home."

"I'm sorry to keep you here," I said. "You can leave any time you want, as far as I'm concerned."

"I can't go back until Frank says so," he said. "I got a job ta do."

"Okay, then," I said, unlocking my car, "maybe we'll go see Frank and get him to send you home."

He shrugged and got in on the passenger side.

"I meant to tell ya before," he said, "this is a nice car."

"Thanks."

"I like Caddies. Had one of my own at home."

"Oh yeah?" I asked. "What kind?"

We talked cars almost all the way to the Sands and as I pulled in behind the building I was thinking Jerry wasn't such a bad guy. At least he had good taste in cars.

I was going to go looking for Frank when we got inside but instead I said to Jerry, "Come on, I'll buy you a drink—that is, unless it's too early for you."

"Ain't never too late for breakfast or too early for a drink," he said. "Not when you grew up in New York where you can get anything any time."

He was proud as hell to be a product of New York. I considered that I'd had a decent upbringing in Brooklyn, but what I remembered most about living there was my job as an accountant, a job I hated.

On the way to the bar we passed a technician working on a slot machine, a porter cleaning out a standing ashtray, a security guard and a handsome man in a tuxedo, all of who greeted me by name.

"Lots of people sure know who you are," Jerry said.

"It's my casino, Jerry," I said. I didn't bother telling him that people in other casinos greeted me, as well. If he stuck with me the way he said he was going to, he'd find that out for himself.

"That fella in the tuxedo . . ." he said.

"Yeah?"

"Was that Vic Damone?"

"It was," I said. "Vic's gonna play the lounge in a couple of days, but he likes to come in early."

Jerry tried not to look impressed.

When we got to the bar I noticed that Beverly wasn't on duty yet. That was good. I didn't want Jerry to scare her.

"What can I get you?" I asked Jerry as we sat at the bar.

"Piels, if ya got it," he said. "Ballantine, if ya ain't."

I told the bartender to bring two Piels.

"So, aren't you curious about what's goin' on, Jerry?" I asked. "I mean, beyond what Frank has told you?"

"No," Jerry said. "If Frank wanted me ta know more he woulda told me."

"And Mr. Giancana? What does he know?"

"Just what Frank told 'im, that he needed somebody here ta help out."

"And that's your job? Helpin' out?"

"It's my job this week, today," Jerry said. "Until it ain't, no more."

"Got a wife waitin' for you at home?"

"Nope."

"A girl?"

"Dames," Jerry said, "but no girl."

"Eddie," the bartender said.

"Yeah?"

"Somebody's been tryin' to get you on the phone. You want me to have it transferred here?"

"Yeah, Harry. Thanks."

A few minutes later Harry brought a phone over and handed the receiver to me.

"This is Eddie."

"Mr. G, it's Mike," Borraco said. "I got somethin' for ya."

"What is it, Mike?"

"I can't tell ya on the phone." He was talking real quick, like he was in a hurry. "Ya gotta meet me."

"Where?"

"Industrial Road." He gave me an address.

"Now, Mike?"

"No, no," Mike said, "tonight, after dark. Like ten P.M."

"Can't we do this sooner—"

"It'll be worth it ta ya, Mr. G," Mike said. "I promise."

"Mike, wait—" I said, but he hung up. I handed the phone back to Harry.

"What was that about?"

"Somebody says he has information for me."

"This somebody. Can you trust 'im?"

"No," I said, "probably not."

"Then I guess I better come with ya."

"You know what, Jerry?" I said. "I think I'd really like that. You want to do any gambling? I can get you a line of credit."

"Naw," Jerry said, "that's okay. I don't gamble, except the ponies."

"You like the horses?" I asked. "We've got time to kill. You any good?"

"I do all right but ya ain't got a track here," Jerry said.

"Jerry," I said, "we got all the tracks here. Come on, my friend."

# *Thirty*

BACK THEN the sports books handled horse racing exclusively, no other sport. They were also off property. I'd often thought the sports books should be brought inside the casinos, where they could be better regulated, and could handle all sports, but that wasn't to happen until about 1968, when Frank "Lefty" Rosenthal came to town with his big ideas. Actually, it would be the idea of a man named Phil Hannifin, who was a commissioner for the state control board, but it would be Rosenthal's testimony before the Gaming Commission that would seal the deal.

So the sports book I took Jerry to was still pretty old-time, with sawdust on the floor and the odds and results posted on black chalkboards. I fixed it so Jerry could play any track he wanted, but he chose to play only the East Coast ones. Belmont, Monmouth, Keystone, they were all running. And I had to admit he did pretty well, and he did it from memory, without doing any handicapping whatsoever.

"I got a good head for horses and jockeys," he told me. "If I was playin' a track I didn't know, like Santa Anita, then I'd need to see the past performances."

Jerry was very animated when he was betting. It wasn't that he shouted to root his horses home, but there was more expression on his face than I had seen at any time during the day.

We killed a good portion of the afternoon playing horses, getting something to eat, and then going back to the horses again so he could try his hand at a few strange tracks. By the time we were done he had made a cool eight grand profit, and was very proud of himself.

"Ya shoulda bet with me, Eddie," he said. "I tol' ya I was good."

"My game is cards, Jerry," I said. "But I'm real happy you did well."

Jerry looked at his watch.

"What time's your meet?"

"Ten P.M."

"Don't it get dark before then?"

"It should be good and dark, Jerry."

We went to the coffee shop for some pie. Beverly still wasn't working. I hadn't seen her all day, so I figured she must have had the day off.

"So, who's this guy yer meetin'?"

"His name's Mike Borraco. You know him?"

"Never heard of him."

"He's local," I said. "Works over at the Riviera."

"Is he a made guy, or what?"

"Mike? No, I think he's just a gopher, but I figured he might have his ear to the ground and be able to pick somethin' up for me."

"You got a lot of made guys in this town?"

When Jerry said "made guy" he got this look in his eye. When a mob guy made his bones by making a hit they said he was "made." I knew Jerry couldn't be made though, because that honor was only bestowed on Italians.

"I suppose so," I answered. "I don't hang out with that crowd, though."

"You work for Mr. Entratter, don't ya?"

"Yeah, I do, but in the casino, Jerry. I don't . . . freelance."

"Well," he said, with a shrug, "that's yer own business, I guess. Just seems to me a smart guy like you could do all right with a little freelancing, ya know? Plus yer Italian."

"All Italians aren't connected, Jerry."

"Guess yer right," Jerry said. "Sure wish I was, though."

"Connected?"

"Italian."

"What's wrong with bein' Jewish?" I asked.

"Nothin'," he said, then added, "if I was workin' in the diamond district, or somethin'."

"What about Meyer Lansky? Seems to me he's doin' okay for himself."

"Mr. Lansky, he's a special case."

I wanted to take the conversation in another direction, and we weren't really getting anything accomplished sitting there.

"We still got a couple of hours to kill before we meet with Borraco," I said. "I think I know how to spend it."

There's "Vegas" and there's "Las Vegas." To me Vegas was the casinos, the action. Las Vegas, on the other hand, was everything else. Homes, stores, restaurants, hotels, bars, clubs, all having nothing to do with the casinos. Consequently most were devoid of mob interests, except for a few bars and strip clubs.

There was a time when I drank a lot, a period of my life I prefer not to think about very often. During that time I frequented a lot of those bars and clubs, and it occurred to me that might be the case with the two men who had ambushed me, Lenny Davis and Buzz Ravisi.

I have to admit having Jerry with me was one of the reasons I felt secure about hitting these places and asking about Davis and Ravisi. I don't know that I would have done it on my own because I sure as hell didn't want to run into those two again when I was flying solo.

We hit two places before I found a bartender I recognized from those drinking days. The place was a strip club where the girls went all the way, which I wasn't even sure was legal. Back when I had frequented the place they'd worked with pasties and G-strings.

The place was dark and smoky, only about half full of men who looked either bored or desperate. As Jerry and I walked past the stage to the bar a topless blonde with bowling-ball tits leaned over and slid her G-string down to her ankles. I took a quick peek, then looked over my shoulder at Jerry to see if he was enjoying the sights. He wasn't. His eyes were combing the room. He'd done the same thing in the other place, watching for trouble. Seeing that a huge set of tits and a bare muff couldn't distract him made me feel even safer.

The bartender did a double take when we reached him.

"Jesus," he said. "Ain't seen you since the night I poured you into a cab. Johnnie Walker Red Label, right?"

"Right," I said.

"That was . . . how long ago was that?"

"A few years."

He smiled, revealing missing teeth in a baby face, remarkable for a man pushing fifty.

"Damn, I got a good memory, right?"

"I hope so."

"Who's your friend?"

"That's Jerry."

I could feel Jerry's hulking presence behind me. He took his job seriously, staying so close to me that no one would have been able to get me from behind.

"You guys wanna drink?"

"Not me," Jerry said. "I'm workin'."

"Scotch?" he asked me.

"No, thanks," I said. "I'm lookin' for a couple of guys."

"You a cop now?" he asked. "I thought you worked for a casino?"

"What's your name again?"

"Marty."

"Look, Marty," I said, "these two guys, they dropped a bundle at my casino and I okayed their credit."

"And they welched?"

"Big time. If I don't find them and get that money I'm out of a job."

"That sucks. Which casino?"

I didn't want him to know where I really worked so I said, "The Flamingo."

"Bugsy's place," he said. "Sounds to me like you might lose more than just yer job."

"That's a real possibility."

He leaned his elbows on the bar.

"Okay, who ya lookin' for?"

"Two guys, usually travel together," I said. "Their names are Buzz Ravisi and Lenny Davis."

The bartender straightened up quick.

"I don't know 'em," he said, and started to back away.

Quicker than I could move Jerry reached out and closed one massive hand around the guy's right wrist.

"Yeah, ya do," he said.

"Hey—"

"If you don't tell me the truth, Marty," I said, "Jerry will break your wrist . . . for starters."

Jerry's hand tightened and Marty's face contorted with pain.

"Awright, awright," he said. "Lemme go."

Jerry didn't let go, but he let up on the pressure some.

"They come in here a lot," he said. "The broad up on the stage now is Buzz's girl."

"The one with the bowling balls?" I asked.

"That's right. Her name's Iris."

I turned and looked at her. She was working the pole, showing the guys her bare ass, bending over to look back between her legs so that her tits hung down and swung like pendulums.

"Have they been in tonight?"

"No," Marty said.

"Last night? The night before?" Jerry asked. "Come on, man." He shook Marty by his wrist.

"Okay, okay," Marty said. "They were in last night, and they should be coming back tonight."

"When tonight?" Jerry asked.

"Midnight," Marty said. "Iris gets off at one. Buzz likes to pick her up, but he likes to watch her work for an hour, first."

"And Davis is always with him?"

"Always," Marty said. "He's got a thing for Iris, too. He's hopin' Buzzy will throw her to him when he's done with her."

"Real friends," Jerry said, releasing his hold on the bartender's wrist.

The bartender started to back away but Jerry stopped him by barking, "Hey!"

"What?"

"If they was to be told we was around askin' about them, I wouldn't like it very much. You understand?"

"Yeah," Marty said, licking his lips, "yeah, I understand."

"You afraid of them fellas?"

"Naw," he said, "naw, I ain't afraid of them . . . exactly. I'm just careful around them."

"You afraid of me?"

Marty stared at Jerry, then lowered his eyes.

"Yeah, just remember that. Okay?"

"Sure, sure," Marty said. "Okay."

"Git lost now."

Marty slunk down to the other end of the bar.

"Whataya wanna do?" he asked.

"We've gotta meet Mike at ten," I said. "Industrial Road's not that far from here. We can get back between twelve and one."

"Yer takin' a chance on missin' these guys."

I looked up at the blonde. She was doing something with her tits I'd never seen before. I wondered how she was able to get them to move in opposite directions like that.

"I guess as long as she's workin' here they'll be back. We can take a chance."

"That's up ta you."

"Maybe I should call the cops," I said. "After all, they did break in and work me over."

"I don't never think you should call the cops, but like I said, that's up to you. If ya do, though you ain't gonna mention Frank, are you?"

"I guess I won't call the cops," I said. I looked at my watch. "If we're gonna meet Mike Borraco we better go now. Then we can hurry back here."

"It's your call," Jerry said. "After all, I'm workin' for you."

Actually, there were a couple of other guys he was working for before me, but I said, "Okay, then let's go."

# Thirty-one

THIS GUY'S AS GOOD as dead."

We'd pulled up in front of a warehouse on Industrial Road when Jerry made his comment. In the dark the building looked like a huge black box—no windows and no lights.

"What are you talking about?"

"I seen enough movies to know what's gonna happen," Jerry said. "He's dead."

"This is real life, Jerry," I said, "not a movie."

"Hey," the big man said, "you got two dead girls already, right? And you got beat up and threatened? Sounds pretty close to me."

"Let's go and find him."

I started to open my door but Jerry put a big paw out to stop me.

"You heeled?"

"No, I'm not heeled," I said, annoyed. "I don't carry a gun. I'm not a cop, a P.I. or a hood."

"Well, I am a hood," he said, "and I'm carryin', so let me go first."

"Look, Jerry," I said over the top of the car, "I'm sorry, I didn't mean—"

"Shhh," he said, waving a huge hand at me. In the other hand he carried his .45; the big gun was still dwarfed by the size of his mitt. "Don't say no more. Let's find this guy."

We approached the warehouse, with me close behind Jerry this time, instead of the other way around.

"Did this guy say where he was gonna be?"

"No," I said, "he just gave me the address."

"Let's jus' find an open door, then."

I followed him around the building. We tried a couple of doors, found them locked and I started to get a bad feeling, like maybe he was right.

The building itself was unmarked. There was no way for us to tell what kind of business was using it, unless there was a sign we couldn't see in the dark.

"I'm gettin' a bad feelin'," Jerry said.

"I thought you had a bad feeling already?"

"It's gettin' worse." He turned to face me. "Look, Mr. Sinatra said I was to keep you safe. I think we better get outta here."

"I think you're right."

We both saw it at the same time. A large trash bin out beside a loading dock. There was just enough moonlight for us to see a flash of red hanging over the edge.

"Your man wear red?" he asked.

"Not the last time I saw him."

I didn't know enough about Mike Borraco to know if red was a favorite color.

"Well, we're here," I said. "We might as well have a look."

As we approached the trash bin I wished I had thought to bring a flashlight. At that moment Jerry reached his empty hand into his pocket and came out with a small pen light. He aimed it at the bin as we got closer. Sure enough, there was a tail end of a red shirt hanging out over the edge.

"You seen a dead body before?" he asked.

"Lots."

He looked at me."

"In the war."

"Korea?"

I nodded.

"I couldn't go," he said. "Flat feet."

"You didn't miss much."

"Want me to take a look, here?"

"No," I said, "we'll stay together."

We walked to the bin and peered over the top. Jerry aimed his pen light inside. Sure enough, Mike Borraco was there, staring back up at us through sightless eyes. His red shirt was torn, the tail end of it having gotten caught on a sharp edge of the metal bin.

"That him?" he asked.

"That's Mike."

Jerry moved the light around. Parts of Mike were buried beneath the garbage.

"I don't see no wound," he said. "I can't tell how he got killed."

"This is crazy," I said. "First the two girls, and now Mike."

"What's this got to do with Mr. Martin?" Jerry asked.

"Nothin'!" I replied. "That's what I'm sayin'. This is all just a crazy coincidence."

"The cops ain't gonna think so, you finding another body. They don't believe in coincidences."

"Well, what am I supposed to do?" I asked. "Not call them?"

"I tol' ya," Jerry said. "Callin' the cops ain't never my first choice."

"So what do you suggest?"

"I suggest we get the hell outta here. There's a chance whoever killed this guy called the cops themselves, hopin' to frame you."

We started for the car and then Jerry stopped and said, "Wait a minute. How did this guy know your phone number?"

"I wrote it down for him. Why?"

He turned and ran back. I saw him reach in and it looked to me like he was rifling the corpse's pockets.

"What are you doing?"

He withdrew his hands and came trotting back to me. He was remarkably light on his feet for such a big man. He handed me a slip of paper I recognized.

"It was in his shirt pocket. Now let's go. We don't want to get caught in the act."

"In the act of what?"

Suddenly, we heard a siren in the distance. Jerry grabbed my shoulder and started pulling me along towards the car.

"In the act of gettin' outta here!"

# Thirty-two

WE MANAGED TO GET OFF of Industrial Road without running into the cops, but I was still uncomfortable about it.

"They're gonna think I'm involved when they find out I was there."

"They're not gonna find out," Jerry said. "That's why I went back for that piece of paper with your number on it."

At the moment that slip of paper was crumpled in one of my pockets where it would do a lot less damage.

"I appreciate what you did, Jerry," I said. "Don't think I don't, but—"

"I was just doin' my job."

He was behind the wheel because I was a little too shaky to drive.

"Where we headed now?"

I checked my watch. It was early enough for us to catch Ravisi and Davis at the strip club, since a dead Mike Borraco had not taken up much of our time.

"I guess we better head back to the club," I said. "At least we can catch up to the two goons who worked me over."

"And then do what?" he asked.

"Huh?"

"When you find them, what're you gonna do?"

"Well, I'm gonna . . ." I realized I hadn't thought that far ahead. "I don't know."

"Find out who they were workin' for when they kicked the crap outta you?"

"Well, yeah."

"And then what?"

"Jerry," I said, "I haven't—"

"I hope you're not thinkin' about turnin' them over to the cops."

"Well . . . yeah, the thought had crossed my mind."

"But not before you find out who they was workin' for, right?"

"Uh . . ."

"And how was you gonna do that, Mr. G? Work'em over yerself?"

"I gotta admit, Jerry," I said, "I haven't exactly thought this through."

"You don't gotta," he said. "That's what I'm here for."

The place was called Club Diamond, a fancy name for what was pretty much a joint. It spoke to how low I'd sunk a few years back that I'd been a regular there.

"Don't get out," Jerry said, grabbing my arm.

"Why not?"

"It's early," he said. "Chances are they ain't here yet. Let's sit out here and see if we can spot 'em."

"What if they *are* already inside?"

"Then we'll catch 'em comin' out. Look, they know you. If they see you inside they're either gonna run, or try ta kill you."

"You have a point."

"And if they try ta kill you," he went on, "I'm gonna have to waste their asses."

"Christ, I don't want you to do that!"

"I know," he said, "but it'd be their choice, not mine."

"So what do we do when they show up?"

"Watch," he said, "wait, and then follow 'em. With a little luck they'll take us home with 'em."

"I really meant it when I said I didn't want to kill them, Jerry."

"I know it," he said. "We're just gonna ask them some questions, that's all."

I stared at his profile, noticed that his hands had tightened on the steering wheel. He noticed it, too, because suddenly he looked at them and let up on the wheel so that the color seeped back into his knuckles.

"This is a nice car," he said.

"Thanks."

"Big enough for me."

"What kind of car do you have at home?"

"I ain't got a car," he said. "I live in Manhattan. Don't need one."

"You must sometimes."

"Oh sure, somebody gives me one when I need it," he explained, "or I rent one." He slid his hands around the wheel, this time lovingly. "Gonna rent one of these next time."

"Jerry," I asked. "What do you do in New York?"

"This and that," he said. "Collections. A lot of collections."

"For loan sharks?"

"Sure, loan sharks. I do pick ups, too. You know, for the boys? Sometimes I gotta get tough, ya know? Break an arm or a leg."

"You like that kind of work?"

"Don't nobody like that kind of work, Mr. G," he said. "It's a job."

We sat quietly for a while, watching the front door of the club. Men came and went, sometimes a man went in with a woman. There were windows with beer signs in them, and above the door the name of the club in blue neon. Vegas was a town of neon, of lights, and it was somebody's job to make sure all the bulbs were on all the time. I sometimes envied whoever had that job. It was so clear what they had to do, with no hidden agendas.

"You ain't thinkin' I'm a hitter, are ya?" Jerry asked, breaking into my reverie.

"What?"

"I ain't no hit man, Mr. G," he said, indignantly.

"I never thought you were, Jerry."

"I've killed people," he went on, "but never for money, and only when they had it comin'."

"And who decided they had it coming?"

"Not me," he said. "I don't make that decision. Because somebody I trust tells me."

I nodded and stared out the window.

"But I ain't no hitter," he said, after a moment.

"I know."

Then he nodded, apparently satisfied that he'd made his point. I didn't see the subtle difference between what he said he did and what he said he didn't do, but that was okay. It worked for him, and that was all that mattered.

"There they are," I said, about half an hour later.

I reached for the door handle and he stopped me again.

"Let them go inside."

We watched as the two men who had broken into my place, beaten me up, kicked and threatened me went into the club.

"Let's go!" I said, too anxious to sit still.

"No."

I looked at him.

"I'll go in. Like I said, they know you."

"You think you can go unnoticed in there?" I asked. "You're a big guy, Jerry."

"With all kinds of tits and ass hangin' out, yeah, I think I can pretty much go unnoticed, but there's one guy I do want to notice me."

"The bartender?"

He nodded.

"I just wanna make sure he keeps his mouth shut."

"How are you going to do that?"

"Just seein' me'll do that." He smiled for the first time since I'd met him. "Like you said, I'm a big guy."

# Thirty-three

LATER, JERRY TOLD ME what happened when he went inside. . . .

He might have thought he could go unnoticed, but that would only be by men. The place was busier than it had been the first time we were there, and there were girls working the floor. A big, healthy-but-tired-looking brunette in a filmy negligee spotted him as soon as he went in and sidled up to him. From the way she moved and looked she was more than a little tipsy.

"Jesus," she said, licking her lips, "you're a big one, aren't you?"

Jerry had heard that a million times before, and since his preference in woman ran to smaller ones he was going to brush her off, but then he thought that would bring him some unwanted attention.

"You're kinda big yerself," he said.

"Double-Ds baby," she said. She pulled down the top of her negligee so that those babies popped out in all their glory. But even the smooth skin and large brown nipples couldn't distract Jerry from what he was there to do. "Listen, we got a room in the back—"

"What's your name, sweetie?" he asked her.

"Catalina."

He knew it wasn't her real name, but that didn't matter.

"They call you Cat?"

"Sometimes." She tucked her tits back in. "You can call me what-ever you want."

"Listen, Cat," he said, "I really need a drink. I was thinkin' of goin' to the bar. How about you and me get together a little later?"

To soften the blow he tucked a ten dollar bill into the soft, smooth valley between her breasts.

"You're on, handsome," she said. "Don't forget about me, though. You'll never know what you missed."

"I won't forget," he lied. "I promise."

I learned that when Jerry was working he had a one-track mind. He just couldn't help it. As soon as he walked away from Catalina and headed for the bar he did just what she asked him not to. He for-got all about her.

But the bartender had not forgotten about him. As he approached the bar the man looked at him and started, as if he thought Jerry might reach across the bar for him. In fact, he backed up a step.

"Where's your partner?"

"Don't matter," Jerry said. "I'm the one you gotta answer to."

"Hey," the man said, "they just came in the door. I ain't said a word to them."

Jerry turned his head and saw the two men sitting at a table, deep in conversation. He knew what they were as soon as he saw him. Two-bitters. They wouldn't last a day in New York.

"They're waitin' for Iris to come out."

"And when does she do that?"

" 'Bout ten minutes. It'll be her last set."

"And then what?"

The man shrugged.

"Then they leave together."

"And go where?"

"Beats me. Her place, their place?"

"Those two live together?"

The bartender snorted.

"Those two do just about everything together—and maybe more, if you know what I mean."

Jerry preferred not to think about what the bartender was talking about.

"Okay," he said. "Keep your nose clean and you won't ever have ta see me again."

"That suits me fine."

Jerry gave him one last look for good measure, then turned and started for the door. Ravisi and Davis had suspended their conversation and were looking at the skinny girl who was finishing up on stage. The big man might have made it out of the place without being seen by them, but at that moment Catalina spotted him heading for the door. She took offense and wasn't shy about letting everybody in the place know it.

"Hey! Big fella! What're ya doin'?" she shouted. "You ain't leavin', are ya? Hey, I'm talkin' to you. I showed you my tits. Nobody leaves after I show 'em my tits."

Jerry thought about simply going out the door as heads turned toward him but then Catalina asked loudly, "What are ya, a faggot or somethin'?"

Well, it wasn't that he got insulted or anything, but he noticed that Ravisi and Davis were among the men looking at him, grinning all the while, and if he just walked out the door after she called him a faggot it wouldn't look right. It would look suspicious.

So what did he do? He walked across the room, put his big hand right up against Catalina's face and shoved her. She went flying, arms pinwheeling, legs going faster and faster as they tried to catch up with her momentum, but to no avail. She slammed into an empty table and both she and the table went to the floor.

"Yeah, big man!" Buzzy Ravisi shouted. "She had it comin'."

Jerry turned and walked out of the club. . . .


"So they saw me," he finished.

"So what?" I asked. "They don't know you were lookin' for them."

"It was just an edge we had that we don't have no more," he said.

"That shouldn't be a problem," I said, hoping I was right.

"No," he said, but he didn't sound like he was in total agreement with me.

About an hour later Ravisi and Davis came out with the blonde, Iris, between them. Even from where we were I could see she was wearing a short skirt and a low-cut top that she was almost falling out of. They walked to a car, an old Chrysler that belched exhaust when they started it.

"They're not gonna be hard to tail," Jerry said, starting the engine. "Hang on."

He waited for them to pull out before putting the Caddy in drive.

"These two are small-timers," he said, as we followed them, "but that don't mean they'll be easy to handle. You sure you don't wanna gun?"

"I'm positive."

"Okay," he said, "but this is what I do, okay? You gotta do what I say when I say it."

"I understand. Just remember, all I want from them is information."

"You'll get it."

"I don't want them killed."

I didn't like the pregnant pause before he said, "I don't kill nobody who ain't got it comin'."

We drove along in silence for a while, following their exhaust cloud, and then Jerry mumbled, "If I was Italian I'd be a made guy, by now."

I didn't know what to say to that.

# Thirty-four

MAYBE WE SHOULD call the cops."

We were sitting in the car in front of a fleabag residential hotel in a rundown section of downtown. Ravisi and Davis had just gone inside with the girl.

Jerry sat as still as a statue at the steering wheel, no expression on his face.

"It's your call," he said, "but you'll have to explain why you didn't call when you first found the body."

"No," I said, "I meant call about these guys, not the body."

"You're convinced they're not connected?"

"I'm positive," I said. "This stuff with the dead bodies, I just walked into that by accident. These guys are involved with whoever is threatening Dino. This is the job I'm supposed to be working on."

"Then you'd have to explain to the cops why you didn't report when they broke into your house and worked you over."

"Shit!" I said. "And I did that to keep both Frank and Dean's name out of the papers."

"Frank don't mind that so much," Jerry said, "but Mr. Martin, that's different."

"Okay, then," I said, "I guess we better go in and get it over with."

Jerry took his .45 out, inspected it, and slid the clip out and in. He worked the slide and looked at me.

"No gun for me."

He raised his eyebrows, shrugged, and slid the .45 into his shoulder holster.

"Let's go," he said.

Of course, I didn't know at the time that Buzz Ravisi had finally decided to share Iris with his partner, Lenny Davis. At that moment they were all getting naked in their hotel room, and Davis's eyes must have been bugging out of his head as he got a look at the naked Iris close up, rather than up on a stage.

Jerry and I entered the hotel lobby and found it empty except for a dozing sixtyish clerk. Jerry walked to the desk and slammed his .45 down on it. The man jumped, saw the gun and gasped. Jerry put a ten-dollar bill next to the gun.

"One of these is gonna get us Buzz Ravisi's room number," he told the man. "It's up to you which one."

"R-room fourteen," the man said. "Second floor."

Jerry glared at the man, then pushed the ten-dollar bill towards him. He picked up his gun, but didn't put it away.

"If you call ahead, me and my friend will be back." Jerry made it clear that he was talking about his gun, and not me.

"Y-yessir."

"Go back to sleep."

The clerk immediately put his head down on the desk. Jerry kept his gun in his hand and headed for the stairs. I followed, my heart pounding because I had no idea what was going to happen when we got into the room.

On the second floor we counted off the rooms and stopped in front of fourteen.

"Now what?" I asked.

"Now we knock," he said, but before I could say a word he lifted his foot and slammed it into the door just above the knob. There was the sound of splintering wood and the door slammed open.

Jerry stepped smoothly into the room, his gun held out in front of him. He blocked my view until he stepped to one side, and then I saw the three naked people on the bed. Ravisi was behind Iris, while Davis was in front of her. Both were at full mast.

Iris, in between them, was on her hands and knees, her breasts dangling down. The tip of Davis' penis was inches from her nose as she turned her head toward the door, her eyes wide with surprise. They were blue, I noticed, because she was staring right at me. I also noticed that I could smell her perfume, along with the mingled odors of sweat and whiskey.

"What the fuck—" Ravisi said.

"Aw, no," Davis said. He'd been just inches from heaven.

"Nobody move," Jerry said.

They didn't move but Ravisi's eyes immediately went to a chair, where both men's shoulder holsters were hanging. It was a good six feet from the bed. There was a small kitchenette off to one side, a sofa and a stuffed chair to the other side.

"Go ahead," Jerry said to Ravisi, "try it."

"W-what's goin' on, Buzz?" Iris stammered.

"Shut up," Ravisi snapped. He looked at Jerry because he had the gun. I didn't even think he'd looked at me once, yet. "What's goin' on?"

"My friend and I have some questions for you and your friend," Jerry said. "Maybe you remember my friend?"

This time he was talking about me, and not his gun. Ravisi looked at me. Davis was still looking down at Iris. Ravisi had slumped to about half mast by now, while Davis's erection was totally gone. Ravisi still had his hands on Iris' ample hips.

Ravisi finally looked at me.

"Aw, shit."

"That's right," I said, "aw shit."

"Look," Ravisi said, "can we move—"

"Naw," Jerry said, "I like you in that position. Just stay that way."

"Mister," Iris said, "can I get dressed and get outta here? I got nothin' to do with this."

"Just stay put, sister," Jerry said. "Don't make me shoot yer tits off."

She bit her lips and a tear started to roll down her cheek. She buried her face on the pillow that was right beneath her head. The move hiked her ass up a little higher. That didn't affect Ravisi but damned if I didn't start to get an erection.

"Look, pal," Ravisi said to me, "no hard feelin's, huh? We was just doin' a job."

"We know that," Jerry said. "What we wanna know is who you did the job for?"

Ravisi licked his lips before he said, "Uh, I can't tell ya that."

"Yeah," Jerry said, "you can. Instead of shootin' off her tits I can start with your balls."

"Hey," Ravisi said, looking at me. Maybe since I wasn't holding a gun he thought he could reason with me.

"Don't plead your case to me, pal," I said. "My ribs are still sore."

"Jesus, Jesus . . ." Davis was mumbling.

"Shut the fuck up!" Ravisi shouted at him.

"Look," Jerry said, "we're real sorry to interrupt your little fuck-fest, here. If you just answer our questions we'll move along and you an yer boyfriend can finish."

"We ain't no faggots!" Ravisi said, anxiously. Then, suddenly, a look of recognition came over his face. "Hey, you're that big guy from the club, what pushed Catalina's face in, ain't ya?"

"That's me."

Ravisi looked from one of us to the other, slowly getting it.

"You were lookin' for us?"

"And we found you," Jerry said. "Like my friend said, his ribs are still sore, and he's real pissed. He wanted me to come in here shootin' but I said no, that you guys would cooperate. After all, you was just doin' a job."

"Right, right," Ravisi said, "we was just doin' a job."

"And that's what I'm doin' now," Jerry said. "A job. And I come all the way from New York to do it."

Ravisi's eyes bugged.

"He imported you from New York?"

"That's right."

The man looked at me with renewed respect.

"You got them kind of connections? You brung in a . . . a pro?"

"That's right," I said, trying to sound tough. "You fucked with the wrong guy."

"Hey, hey," Davis whined, "we didn't know you was connected."

"Yeah," Ravisi said, "all we knew was—"

"You knew he worked at the Sands, didn't ya?" Jerry asked.

"Well, yeah—"

"And who runs the Sands?"

"Well—"

"Look," Jerry said, "you guys made a mistake. It happens. We're willin' to overlook it."

"You are?" Ravisi asked. He looked directly at me.

"Well . . . yeah," I was, grudgingly, "but I need some answers."

Iris still had her head in the pillow, but I could tell she was crying because her dangling tits were jiggling.

"Let her go," I said.

"What?" Jerry asked, without looking at me.

"Let the girl go."

She lifted her head from the pillow and turned her tear streaked face towards me.

"Okay," Jerry said, "get up, sweetheart. Get dressed and get out of here."

Without hesitation Iris leaped from the bed, ample flesh jiggling everywhere now as she got dressed in a hurry. No underwear, she just pulled on her top and her skirt and slipped into her high heels.

"Hey, sister," Jerry said.

"W-what?"

"No cops."

"I ain't callin' the cops," she said. "I swear."

"Go on," I said. "Get lost."

She put her hand on my arm and said, "Thanks, Mister. You come by the club some night and I'll pay ya back."

"Sure."

She turned to look at Ravisi then and spat, "And don't you come by no more—and don't ever call me."

"Hey, what'd I do?" he demanded.

"You almost got me killed!"

"Iris—"

She turned and stormed out of the room, high heels clacking down the hall.

"Goddamn it," Lenny Davis said, and he was almost crying as the sound of Iris's heels faded away.

"Shut up!" Ravisi said. He looked at Jerry. "How about us? Can we get dressed?"

"Naw," Jerry said. "You guys stay just like you are. We're gonna have us a talk."

# Thirty-five

THE SITUATION WAS STRANGE, to say the least. Four men in the room, two naked on the bed and one holding a gun. The fourth one—me—wasn't sure what was going to happen next.

"This ain't right," Davis said.

"Shut up!" That came from both Ravisi and Jerry.

"You guys can walk away from this real easy," Jerry told them. "Just tell my friend who hired you to work him over and warn him off."

"Warn him off of what?" Ravisi asked. "We don't even know what we was warning him off of."

"How's that?" I asked.

"Look," Ravisi said, "we got hired over the phone, and we picked up our pay at a drop. That's it."

"And what were you told to do?" Jerry asked.

"Work this guy over," Ravisi said, indicating me with an impatient wave.

Jerry looked at me, the first time he took his eyes off the two men. Ravisi took the opportunity to move. He lunged for the top of the bed, sliding his hand beneath one of the pillows. I could only think that he was going for a hidden gun.

"Jerry!"

The big man's head snapped back around as Ravisi's hand was coming out from under the pillow. Jerry squeezed the trigger of the big .45. The bullet struck Ravisi in the chest and splattered the wall behind him with blood and guts. The gun in the hood's right hand went off and a .38 slug hit Davis in the left temple and splashed his brains all over the sheets.

"Jesus!" I shouted. "Christ!"

"Take it easy," Jerry said.

He stepped to the bed and swept the snub-nosed .38 to the floor, then checked both men before holstering his own gun.

"Are they dead?" I asked.

"Can't get any deader."

"Christ," I said, again. My chest felt tight, like I was having a heart attack, and I'd broken out in a sweat. Jerry looked over at me, then got right in my face and slapped me—not hard, but hard enough.

"Breathe," he said.

"Huh?"

"Come on," he said, "Deep breaths."

I took a deep breath and let it out.

"Another one."

I did it again, and again. Suddenly, the steel band around my chest was gone. I still felt hot, but at least I could breathe.

"Okay?" he asked. "Are you okay?"

"Yeah," I said, "yeah. I think so."

"We have to look around," he said, "but don't leave your fingerprints anywhere."

"What?"

"We have to search the place and then get outta here before the cops come."

"W-what are we lookin' for?"

"Anythin' that will tell us who these two were workin' for. Come on, Mr. G. The place ain't that big."

We went through the place as thoroughly as we could and as fast as we could. The clerk might have called the cops, or maybe the girl had, before the shooting. Certainly someone must have called them after the shots, but I still didn't hear any sirens. I was careful to keep my eyes averted from the bed, which was soaking through with the blood of both men. I'd had enough of dead bodies in the past couple of days to last me a lifetime. Watching the lead rip through these two right in front of me was more than enough.

"Find anything?" Jerry asked.

"No." I'd picked up a pen from somewhere and was using it to open drawers and go through things, even underwear. "You?"

"I got a phone book and calendar," he said.

"Anythin' on it?"

"I don't know." He shoved it into his pocket. "Let's get out of here."

I started to put down the pen I was using, then thought better of it and shoved it in my pocket.

"You touch anything?" he asked.

"I don't think so."

"Ya gotta be sure," Jerry said. "From the minute we came in, did you touch anything?"

"No," I said, "no. You kicked open the door, so . . . no."

"Then let's get out of here."

As we went through the lobby I noticed that the clerk still had his head down on the desk. He'd either stayed that way the whole time, or had assumed the position when he heard us coming down the stairs.

In the car Jerry got behind the wheel again.

"What about the clerk?" I asked. "Or the girl?"

"What about them?"

"Either one can identify us."

"They won't say a word."

"Why not?"

"Fear," he answered. "In my business, it's my best friend. Come on, gimme some directions."

"Where to?"

"I don't know," he said. "We might as well go back to your place. I think we're done for the night, don't you?"

"More than done," I agreed.

\* \* \*

When we got to my place we approached it slowly, carefully. I didn't know if we were expecting more goons, or the cops. I didn't want anyone to be there because I needed to sit quietly, have a beer and think.

Once we were inside and established that we were alone I grabbed two bottles of Piels from the refrigerator, handed one to Jerry, and then went to sit on the sofa in the living room. Jerry chose the big, overstuffed armchair across from me.

"I'm sorry," I said to him.

"What for?"

"That you had to kill those men."

"I didn't kill both of 'em," he said. "I killed one and he killed the other one."

"Whichever way it went—"

"And there ain't nothin' for you to be sorry about," he went on. "The idiot went for a gun. I'm sorry I had to kill 'im before we got what you were after."

"You didn't believe them?"

"What? That they got hired on the phone and picked up their money from a drop?" he shrugged. "Could be. It ain't the way I would work, but these two weren't real pros."

"Well," I said, "I'm back to square one. At least with them warning me off I had somebody to go lookin' for; I had a reason to believe that the threats made to Dean Martin were real."

"Look on the bright side," he said.

"What's the bright side?"

"With those two dead," he said, "whoever hired them is gonna have to hire somebody new to go after you."

"To go after—you mean—"

"They ain't about to let it go," Jerry said. "You got beat up and threatened off and you still kept goin'. Next time, they're gonna try harder."

Christ. I hadn't thought of that.

# Thirty-six

JERRY DECIDED TO STAY the night on the couch instead of going back to the Sands, where he had a suite. Briefly, I had considered both of us going back to the Sands, but he said he thought I'd have a few days grace until whoever hired Ravisi and Davis found out about their deaths and then replaced them.

When I got up the next morning I could smell coffee. Jerry already had the percolator going, and something in the toaster as I entered the kitchen.

"All you had was bread," he said, "so I'm makin' some toast."

"We could've gone out for breakfast," I said.

"We still can," he said. "I just have to have somethin' in the mornin' before I get started."

"Did you sleep okay?" I asked.

"You mean because I killed somebody last night?" he asked.

"No," I said, "because you slept on the couch, which is too small for you."

"I managed," he said.

We sat at the table together, buttered our toast and ate, washing it down with sips of good, strong black coffee. It struck me that this was the second time in as many days that a man had come to my house and made me coffee.

We exchanged some inane conversation for a few minutes, getting to know each other a little better. I found out that he liked watching westerns on TV—*Bonanza, Gunsmoke, Maverick*—but that his favorite TV show was *The Untouchables*. I told him I preferred the Warner Bros. private-eye shows like *77 Sunset Strip, Hawaiian Eye, The Untouchables* and *Bourbon Street Beat*.

"Them shows are too phony for me," he said. "I mean, westerns is history, and so is *The Untouchables*. Those other shows poke fun at mugs like me. That Kookie, fer instance? I woulda made him eat that comb of his a long time ago. I prefer more realistic characters."

I stared at him for a moment, surprised.

"I ain't as dumb as I sound, Mr. G," he said. "That's just what a heavy Brooklyn accent does ta ya. You managed to get rid of yours. I get the feelin' you wasn't on the streets as long as I was."

That was true enough. I'd gone to college, gotten my degree and became a CPA.

"So whatta you wanna do today?" he asked.

"To tell you the truth I'd like to just go back to work and forget everything else."

"You could do that?" her asked. "Tell Frank and Mr. Martin that?"

"No," I said. "I told them I'd help. I can't go back on my word."

"So you really think this other stuff is separate?" he asked.

"It's got to be," I said.

"How'd you get involved in it?"

I'd been intending to think it over that morning, so maybe talking it out with Jerry would be even better.

"Look," I said, "let's finish up here and then I'll take you somewhere for breakfast and we can talk it out."

"I ain't much for talkin'," he said, "but I'm a good listener."

"Great. That's what I need right now."


I took Jerry to a small diner near my place where I sometimes had breakfast before going to work, or on my days off. He ordered pancakes, scrambled eggs, bacon, potatoes, coffee and juice. While we hadn't exactly had breakfast together yesterday, we'd had it in the same place, so I knew he ate big. The only other meal I'd had with him had been dinner the day before at the Sands, where he'd consumed a twenty-ounce prime rib in record time along with vegetables, a salad and a couple of loaves of bread.

"How tall are you?" I asked, when we had our food.

"I go about six-five, and about two-eighty. I've been over three hundred pounds, but that makes me feel sluggish."

I ordered a more normal size omelet, juice and coffee.

"You was gonna tell me how you got mixed up with them dead girls," he reminded me.

I told him how I'd been stumped about how to move forward with the Dean Martin thing, so I'd thought of going to find Lou Terazzo to see if he knew anything.

"This Terazzo, he's in a family?"

"Yeah, he works over at the Riviera."

Jerry nodded and shoveled some pancakes into his mouth.

I told him about locating Terazzo's girl and how she had run out on me, how I tracked her down to where she lived and found her roommate in the pool.

"And then she turns up dead, too."

"Only you didn't find her?"

"No," I said, "the cops filled me about that one."

I back tracked, then, and told him how Mike Borraco had gotten involved.

"And then he ends up dead."

"Right."

Jerry sopped up the rest of his eggs with some toast, stuffed it into his mouth and then sat back with a contented sigh.

"So if you hadn't gone lookin' for this Unlucky Lou guy in the first place, you probably wouldn't know nothin' about these dead girls."

"Probably not."

He raised his eyebrows.

"What are you thinkin'?" I asked.

"Well, I tol' ya I ain't much for talkin, and I'm probably even less for thinkin', but it occurs to me to wonder if those girls woulda ended up dead if you hadn't gone looking for Unlucky Lou in the first place?"

"So you're sayin' I could be the link between the two things?"

"Do you see another link?"

"Well, I didn't see any link . . . until now."

"Did you tell anyone why you was lookin' for Terazzo? What you was gonna ask 'im?"

I thought back, but I couldn't remember.

"I'm not sure, but even if I had, just because I was askin' questions about somebody threatening Dean Martin . . . I don't see how that blows up into murder."

"Well, you asked this Borraco guy to find Terazzo for ya, and now he's dead. I ain't tryin' ta make you feel bad, Mr. G, but you sure do seem to be the link, here."

I sat back and thought a moment, then leaned forward and said, "If that's the case, Jerry, then I'm even more confused."

"I don't blame ya," he said, and burped. A mixture of odors— mostly syrup and meat—wafted across the table at me.

"I think I should go to the cops," I said, abruptly.

"What for?"

"To make sure they don't come lookin' for me. I'll call the detective in charge, or go and see him, and ask what he's found out about the girls. I figure they'll think if I had somethin' to hide I wouldn't be goin' to see them."

Jerry considered it for a moment, then said, "That sounds like a smart idea, Mr. G. But if you go to the cops I can't go with ya. I hope you understand."

"I understand, Jerry. You can wait at the Sands. I'll do it this morning and get it over with."

# Thirty-seven

A HARNESS BULL walked me through the building until we reached a squad room. Detective Hargrove looked up from his desk as we approached and showed no surprise at seeing me there. He said something to his partner, Smith, who was sitting across from him. When the Negro turned and looked at me he did look surprised.

"Mr. Gianelli," Hargrove said. "To what do we owe this pleasure? Thank you, Officer."

The cop nodded and left. Neither Hargrove or his partner offered me a chair.

"I was just wondering if you've found out anything about the two dead girls."

"Why are you concerned?" Hargrove asked. "You said you didn't know either of them."

"Well, I did find the first one, though," I pointed out. "I kind of feel . . ."

"Responsible?" Smith asked.

"No," I said, "not at all."

"Just curious, then," Hargrove said.

"Well, it's a little more than that."

"Unfortunately," Hargrove said, "we don't have much to tell you.

We still haven't located the second girl's boyfriend, Lou Terazzo. You haven't seen him, have you, Mr. Gianelli?"

"No, I haven't."

"I guess you're still pretty upset about him owing your casino money."

"The Sands is very concerned."

"Can that kind of thing cost you your job?' Smith asked.

"It might."

"Too bad."

"We have found something, though," Hargrove said. "Maybe you can help us with this."

"What is it?"

"Do you know a man named Mike Borraco?"

I frowned, like I was trying to place the name.

"Doesn't he work at the Riviera?"

"That's right, he does," Hargrove said. "I figured since you both work for casinos you might know him."

"Not well," I said. "What's he done?"

"Got himself killed."

I tried to look surprised, but I felt silly doing it and wondered if they could tell.

"How?"

"Somebody slipped a knife into his back," Smith said. "Nice and neat, dumped his body in the garbage. Sheriff's deputies found him early this morning."

"Jesus."

"Yeah," Hargrove said, "third employee of the Riviera to be killed in a couple of days. Looks like somebody might have it in for the Riv."

"That's too bad."

"Hope your buddy Terazzo doesn't show up dead," Hargrove said. "That'd be really bad for your casino."

"We'd have to write the debt off."

"Say, I just realized something," Hargrove said.

I didn't know if he was talking to me or his partner, so I just kept my mouth shut.

"What's that?" his partner asked.

"Didn't Mr. Gianelli here tell us when we first interviewed him that he worked for the Flamingo, Jake?" Hargrove looked very puzzled.

"I think he did, Mike. Why?"

"Well . . . just a minute ago he said he worked for the Sands."

Hargrove and his partner both looked at me. I did some fast thinking? Had I lied about where I worked when I spoke to them the first time? I didn't think so. Was he trying to rattle me?

"No," I said, "I think when you first interviewed me I said the Sands."

"Really?" Hargrove asked, frowning. "I don't usually make mistakes like that, do I, Jake?"

"No, Mike, you sure don't."

"I could check my notes," he said. "See what I wrote down that first time." He looked at me. "Should I check my notes, Mr. Gianelli?"

"I suppose so, Detective," I said. "I guess one of us mighta made a mistake."

"Oh, you mean you might have said the Flamingo when you meant the Sands?"

Right at that moment I remembered that I had lied about where I worked, but not to the cops. I'd told the bartender in the strip club that I worked at the Flamingo, not wanting him to know where I really worked.

"No," I said, "now that I think about it, I said the Sands. I wouldn't have had any reason to say something else."

"That's what I was thinkin'," he said. "Why would you lie about where you worked?"

"I wouldn't," I said. "That would be too easy for you to check."

"He's got you there, Mike," Smith said.

"Yeah, he does," Hargrove said. "Why would he lie, indeed?"

I had the feeling they were toying with me, but I stuck to my guns.

"Anyway," Hargrove said, "do you know of any reason this Lou Terazzo would kill all these people, Mr. Gianelli?"

"Lou? You think he killed them?"

"Well, he's missing," Hargrove said. "Until he shows up dead, too, he makes a pretty good suspect. Maybe Borraco was making time with Terazzo's girl?"

"I'm afraid I don't know any of 'em well enough to say, Detective, but you gotta wonder about a girl who would cheat on Lou with a man like Mike."

"Yeah, you're right," Hargrove said. "Borraco was a little weasel."

"I don't think I can be very much help."

"I guess not," Hargrove said, "but there was no harm in asking. I mean, you came down here to try and help, right?"

"Uh, yeah," I said, "I did. I mean, I was curious, like you said, but I could help—"

"We'll let you know, Mr. Gianelli," Smith said. "If we need your help, I mean."

"Yeah," Hargrove said, "thanks for comin' down."

"Sure," I said, "sure."

"We'll keep you informed," he went on, "I mean, seein' as how you found the first girl and all. Just as a courtesy."

"I appreciate it."

Smith turned his chair so he was no longer facing me. I looked at Hargrove, but he'd found something on his desk to occupy him, so I turned and left.


Outside, on the front steps, I found Danny Bardini waiting for me.

"What are you doin' here?" I asked.

"I might ask you the same thing," he said. "Are you nuts?"

"I might be," I said. "Why don't we find someplace to talk and maybe we can figure it out?"

# Thirty-eight

WE STAYED OFF THE STRIP and away from Fremont Street, went to a local bar we both knew we'd be left alone at. It was early, so the place wasn't very full.

"I went to the Sands lookin' for you," he said, when we both had a beer in front of us. "Some big goon named Jerry gave me the third degree until I told him who I was and showed him my ID."

I'd mentioned Danny to Jerry, figuring they were going to meet, eventually.

"Yeah, he was a gift from Frank, to watch my back."

"I could watch your back."

"I didn't want to tell Frank no."

"How's the guy workin' out?"

I told him about everything I'd gone through in just one day with Jerry.

"I guess he's workin' out, then," Danny said, "just remember, he ain't really workin' for you."

"I know."

"He told me you went to the cops," Danny said. "What'd you tell them?"

"Nothing," I said. "I just wanted them to know I was around.

Seems that because Lou Terazzo is missin', he's the number one suspect."

"What do you think is goin' on?"

"I don't know, Danny," I said. "I still don't think all the killings have anything to do with the threats against Dean Martin, but I guess I could be wrong."

"Sounds to me like you just walked into the middle of somethin'."

"So how do I get out of it?"

"Damned if I know. I was lookin' for you all day yesterday to tell you I thought I'd located Buzz Ravisi. Guess you didn't need me for that."

"I appreciate the work, anyway," I said. I told him how Jerry and I had come to follow Ravisi and Davis home with the girl, Iris.

"As long as the girl and the clerk stay quiet you shouldn't have any trouble."

"As long as they're afraid of Jerry. . . ." I started, then stopped. I shook my head as the scene from last night replayed itself in my head.

"I saw men get shot in the war, Danny, but never anything that close up, you know?"

"I know," Danny said. "I've seen it. Lead is unforgiving when it meets flesh and bone."

"I didn't pull the trigger," I went on, "but it's my fault those two are dead. If I hadn't been lookin' for them—"

"Hey," Danny said, "they deserved it." He looked around, made sure no one was sitting within earshot of our spot at the bar. "Believe me, those two have done worse than kick your ass."

I held up two fingers to the bartender and he brought over two more drafts.

"Look," Danny said, "my advice is to just forget about Lou Terazzo and those killings and concentrate on your main objective—finding out who's threatening Dean Martin."

"You're right."

He downed half his second beer and then set the bottle on the bar with a bang.

"That's it for me. As it is I'll have to explain to Penny why I smell like beer so early in the day. Where are you headed?"

"Back to the Sands."

"To hook up with Jerry?"

"To start from scratch," I said. "You go ahead. I'm gonna finish my beer."

He stood up and slapped my shoulder.

"Don't worry about anything," Danny said. "So far you're not implicated in or suspected of anything."

"It's the 'so far' that worries me," I said.

After he left I finished my beer, then kept the bartender from removing the remainder of his and drank that, too.

When I got to the Sands it wasn't hard to spot Jerry. I walked through the casino, waved absently at some players and co-workers, and then saw him sitting in the lounge, watching the floor. He spotted me as I approached, but remained where he was and let me come to him.

"Did your P.I. friend find you?" he asked.

"Yeah," I said. "Danny Bardini. A good friend of mine."

"I know," Jerry said. "I remember you tellin' me. That's why I tol' him where you was."

"I appreciate it."

"Did he have somethin' for ya?"

I told Jerry that Danny had located Ravisi, but we were already past that.

"How'd things go with the cops?"

"They're looking for Lou Terazzo," I said. "They like him for the murders."

"The two girls?" he asked.

"They found Mike Borraco," I said. "They're thinkin' maybe Carla was two-timin' Lou with him, but I don't buy that."

"So you don't like him for it?"

"Not for that reason," I said.

"It's a pretty good reason," Jerry told me. "It's usually true more times than it ain't."

"Nah," I said, "not this time. Lou's a ladies' man, and Mike just isn't."

Jerry shrugged. None of it really mattered to him.

"So whattaya gonna do?"

"What I set out to do in the first place," I said. "My only problem is knowing where to go from here."

"I might be able to help you with that."

"Oh? How's that?"

"I talked to Frank today," Jerry said. "He wants you to come to the set."

"The set?" I asked. "Of *Ocean's Eleven?*"

"That's what they're shootin', ain't it?"

"Why would he want me to come to the set?"

"I didn't ask him," Jerry said. "I'm just passin' on the message."

I checked my watch. It was almost one.

"Will they still be shootin' now?"

"They're still there. I'm supposed to take you over." He stood up from his barstool, towered above me. I had the distinct feeling I didn't have a choice.

"Well, okay, then," I said. "Let's go watch 'em shoot *Ocean's Eleven.*"

# Thirty-nine

I WATCHED AS FRANK SINATRA, Dean Martin, Sammy Davis Jr. and Peter Lawford shot a scene around a pool table. Off to one side sat Henry Silva on a sofa with an actor named Richard Benedict. Joey Bishop, Richard Conte, Buddy Lester and Norman Fell sat at a table, supposedly playing gin. I looked around in vain but did not see Angie Dickinson anywhere. Akim Tamiroff was standing off to one side, watching, waiting for his cue to stalk around the room, mug and grunt. They were pretty much dressed alike, jackets and shirts with ties.

The room was set up as an expensive rumpus room in a Beverly Hills home. Sinatra was playing "Danny Ocean," who had gathered all eleven of the men who were in his unit in World War II, the 82nd Airborne, to Las Vegas to knock off five casinos. That was the basic premise of the film *Ocean's 11*.

At the moment the cameras were on Sinatra, Dino, Sammy Davis and Peter Lawford, who were having an inane conversation around the pool table about what they would each do with their take from the job. I noticed that all but Peter Lawford were holding a cigarette along with their pool cue.

Peter Lawford was talking about buying votes and making himself into a politician while the others made fun of him. Lawford was rich boy "Jimmy Foster," who was tired of asking his mother for money every time he needed it. Dino was Ocean's closest friend, "Sam Harmon." That part seemed true to life. All I heard them call Sammy in that scene was "Josh."

Director Lewis Milestone called "Cut and print," but he didn't look happy. From what brief by play I had seen between him and Sinatra it was clear that Frank was calling the shots.

"Let's set up for the next scene," Milestone called out.

Frank walked over to Dean, said something and then the two crooners started over towards me. My heart thumped faster, and I started to sweat. I had nothing solid to report to them, and knew I was going to disappoint them. I was also upset that Sammy wasn't coming with them. I wanted to meet him. I didn't care to meet Lawford. He struck me as a hanger-on with not an ounce of the talent the other three had, but it was my understanding that he had brought the script to Sinatra. I also figured out, from the papers and scuttlebutt around the Sands, that he was Frank's connection to John F. Kennedy and his whole family. Sinatra was a big Kennedy booster and was trying his best to help JFK get into the White House as the first Irish Catholic President of the United States.

But that was politics, and I hated politics.

"Eddie," Sinatra said, as they reached me. He put a friendly hand on my shoulder.

"Hello, Eddie," Dean Martin said, shaking my hand.

"Frank," I said, "Dean." I didn't know what else to say. I was wondering why I had been brought there, to the *Ocean's 11* set?

"We only have a few minutes," Frank said. "We have to shoot another scene around the pool table."

"We heard you've had a rough couple of days," Dean said.

"You heard?" I asked, before I realized they must have heard it from Jerry.

"What's this other thing you've gotten involved in?' Frank asked. "A couple of dead broads?"

"And a dead guy," I said. "He worked at the Riviera . . . but I'm not involved."

"You found one of the girls, didn't you?" Frank asked.

"I did," I said, "but I was lookin' for a guy I know, who might have had some information about . . ." I lowered my voice and looked around. ". . . you know, that thing we talked about."

"So those broads are connected to our problem?" Frank asked. "Can we expect the police to visit us?"

"No," I said. "I haven't mentioned either of your names to the them."

"Why not?" Dean asked. "Seems to me it might have made things easier for you."

"That may be," I said, "but I didn't think you wanted me to, and I also don't think the two things were related."

"So you haven't told the police anything about us?" Frank asked.

"No, Frank, I haven't."

Frank looked at Dean and said, "I told you he was a stand-up clyde."

"Did Jerry tell you, well, everything that happened?" I asked.

"Yeah, he did," Frank said. "I guess you're pretty happy with my gift, eh?"

"Well," I said, "considering he probably saved my life, yeah."

"Look, we have to shoot this scene," Frank said. "Dean and I wanted you here so we could tell you we'll understand if you want to pull out."

"Sounds like you've had a pretty crazy time," Dean said.

"I've had more excitement in the past two days than I've had in a lifetime."

Frank looked amused.

"And that's a good or a bad thing?"

"I'll have to let you know, Frank," I said. "Look, I appreciate the opportunity to pull out, but I think I'll pass. I still want to help."

"Keep Jerry with you, pally," Dean said. "I don't want anything to happen to you on my account."

"Have you had anymore notes?" I asked him.

"No, nothing since we talked."

"No calls?"

He shook his head.

"I don't see any extra security around," I said. There was a guard on the door when we arrived, but he had stepped aside and let us enter.

"We don't want anybody askin' questions about bodyguards," Frank said. "We all made sure we were with Dean on the way here, and Nick and Henry and I will be takin' him back to the Sands."

"I'm not sure what—"

"There's the director," Frank said, cutting me off. "He's already pissed off at me, so we better go and shoot this scene."

Dean put his hand on my shoulder and said, "Take care."

They turned and walked back to the pool table. I noticed that all the actors had stood and were approaching the table, including one guy I hadn't noticed before, a blond man with large ears I later found out was named Clem Harvey.

I stayed and watched the scene, and at the end of it they all placed their hands in the center of the table, one on top of the other. When Sammy Davis placed his hand on the pile last Lewis Milestone once again yelled, "Cut and print!"

"We better go," Jerry said, looming behind me and speaking in my ear.

I nodded and we headed for the door.

# Forty

JERRY LIKED MY CADDY so much that I'd let him drive again. He'd gotten directions to the shoot, so I didn't pay attention while he drove. Now that we were outside I suddenly realized where we were.

"Oh," I said, "this is bad."

"What?" he asked. "What's bad?"

"That's Industrial Road," I said, pointing.

"So?"

"Get in the car. You drive."

We got in and he started the engine.

"Drive around the building."

He did as I asked, circling the building until I said stop.

"Look familiar?" I asked.

"No."

"Look around."

He did, craning his neck. I watched the expression on his face, which was usually pretty blank. In the short time since we'd met we'd spent a lot of time together. I was able to tell when he realized something was wrong.

"I get it."

"That trash bin over there," I said. "That's where we found Mike Boracco."

We could still see the flash of red from the piece of Boracco's shirt that had gotten torn off.

"Okay," I said, "get us out of here."

"Where to?"

"Binion's," I said. "Let's go to Binion's. They've got a killer coffee shop and I have to think."

I gave him directions.


When we got to the Horseshoe, Jerry remembered that was where he'd had the two dozen pancakes.

"They were good."

"Have some more," I suggested, even though we already had breakfast.

"I think I will."

He ordered the pancakes and I ordered a turkey sandwich on toast with fries. We shared a booth—well, actually, we didn't share it. He took up two thirds of it.

"So what's it mean?" he asked.

"You're not as dumb as you seem, remember?" I asked.

He smiled again, only the second time since I'd met him.

"Everything is connected."

"I don't know how it got that way," I said, "but yeah, everything is connected. Look, sit tight. I'm gonna call Danny Bardini and have him join us. He can walk here from his office."

"Fine with me," he said. "I hate cops, but I got nothin' against P.I.'s. They're workin' stiffs, just like the rest of us."

I left him there with the waitress pouring us each coffee and went to the pay phone. The coffee shop was on the lower level, underneath the casino, so there was no noise in or around the booth. I got Penny, who put me through to Danny, who said he'd be right over as long as I was buying.

When I got back to the booth Jerry had already started on his pancakes, and my sandwich was waiting for me.

"Get 'im?" he asked around a mouthful.

"He'll be here in a minute."

"You go back a way with him?"

"His brother was my best friend in Brooklyn, when we were growing up."

"That's a long ways," he said. "I got nobody from when I was a kid. Everybody's gone."

"That's too bad."

"Maybe."

Jerry still had a dozen to go when Danny arrived. He used his detective skills and immediately deduced that he couldn't fit into the booth, so he pulled a chair over and sat on the outside.

"You guys already met," I said.

"Yeah," Danny said. "This mornin' at the Sands. How are ya?"

Jerry nodded.

The waitress came over and Danny ordered a burger platter.

"What's up?"

I told him about going to the *Ocean's 11* set and then finding out that it was inside the warehouse where we'd found Mike Borraco.

"So everything is connected," he said.

"I'm afraid so."

"Unless it's just a coincidence."

"Borraco just happens to ask me to meet him outside the building that houses *Ocean's Eleven*? I don't think so."

"How much of the movie is being shot here?"

"They're supposed to shoot for eleven days. This is day three, I think. Then they go back to Hollywood to finish."

"So if Dean Martin makes it through the next eight days he should be okay. Or, at least, out of Las Vegas. Did he receive any threats before he arrived?"

"No," I said, "only here."

"So something's gonna happen in the next eight days," Danny said.

"Unless they're just threats," Jerry said.

"Well," Danny replied, "the fact that two guys worked Eddie over would make it more than just threats, I think."

Jerry eyed Danny carefully, I had not told him that I'd filled Danny in on the whole story, and that Danny knew he'd killed Buzz

Ravisi. But now Jerry knew how far back Danny and I went, he could probably guess. I wondered if I'd just put Danny in a bad spot. I trusted him, but why should Jerry?

"You got a point," Jerry said, and went back to his last half-dozen pancakes.

The waitress brought Danny his burger platter. It would have made any Brooklyn diner proud. Burger, bun, lettuce, tomato, red onion and large pickle slices. And fries. Danny assembled it all and took a bite.

"I suppose you're not goin' to the cops with this information?"

"No," I said, "no cops."

"So it's just the three of us who know, huh?"

"Unless the cops check out that warehouse and find out it's being used to film a movie."

"Danny shook his head.

"That wouldn't get them to the Rat Pack," he said. "Just to the producers."

"So okay," I said, "only the three of us know that all the killings are somehow related to the threats on Dean Martin's life. And also, maybe, to the filming of *Ocean's Eleven*."

"Now the question remains," Danny said. "What do we do with this knowledge?"

"You guys are the pros," I said. "Help me out here. Suggest something."

Jerry looked at me, jerked his head towards Danny and said, "He's the P.I. He's a pro. Me, I'm just muscle sent by Frank to keep you safe."

"And doin' a helluva job, from what I hear," Danny said.

Jerry did not look like he appreciated the compliment.

# *Forty-one*

WELL," DANNY SAID, "as a pro I'd say you've got somebody inside the Sands workin' on this."

The waitress had cleared the table and we were all having coffee.

"I talked to the staff," I said, "especially the people on the front desk."

"Eddie," Danny said, "somebody's lying to you. Somebody saw somethin' they're not tellin' you, or did somethin' they're not tellin' you. What you have to do is find out who and what it is."

"I can help with that," Jerry said.

"How?" I asked.

"Just let me pound on some people until they talk."

"I think I'll save that as a last resort, Jerry," I said.

"It usually works," he grumbled.

"My guess would be it's someone who was recently hired," Danny went on. "Maybe because they knew that Frank and Dino and the others would be here. There have been no threats against the others? Sammy Davis? Joey Bishop? No Jew bashing? No bigots because Sammy's a Negro?"

"Nothin'," I said. "Just Dean."

"If it was Peter Lawford it could even be political, since he's part of the Kennedy clan."

"Not a peep," I said, "unless they're not tellin' me."

We all sat there in silence for a few moments. The only sound was Jerry chewing the last of his pancakes, washing it down with the final swigs of coffee.

"Why would they not tell you?" Danny asked. "Why tell you about Dean Martin and not the others?"

"It doesn't make sense."

"Unless," Jerry said, "the others have had threats and are clammin' up about it."

Danny and I looked at him.

"Why would they not say anythin'?"

Jerry shrugged.

"Maybe Sammy Davis is so used to threats he doesn't mention them," Danny offered.

"And maybe Lawford does think they're political, and have nothin' to do with Vegas," I said.

"Have you met them yet?" Danny asked.

"No," I said. "And I've been wanting to meet Sammy. I only know Joey, Frank and Dino, right now. I've been introduced to Richard Conte and Henry Silva—"

"Angie Dickinson?" Danny asked, hopefully.

"Not yet."

"Well, Conte and Silva, they're just actors, not really part of the Rat Pack."

"Frank is the only one who was part of the original Rat Pack," Jerry said.

"That's right," Danny said. "I read about that. It was Humphrey Bogart and Lauren Bacall who started it. After Bogie died, Frank sort of took it over, changed some of the members—"

"He calls it the Summit," Jerry said. Again, we looked at him. "The newspapers, they stuck them with the Rat Pack name. Frank even tried callin' it the Clan."

"That wouldn't fly in the papers," Danny said. "Not with Sammy as a member."

I waved at the waitress and made a writing motion in the air, asking for the check.

"Seems like I suddenly have a lot to do," I said.

"Do you know somebody in employment at the Sands?" Danny asked. "They could get you a list of recent employees."

"And then I'll have to interview all of them," I said. I looked at Danny. "I don't suppose you'd be interested—"

"I'll interview Angie Dickinson," he said. "Or even Shirley Maclaine. I hear she's got a bit part."

I stared at him.

"Look, I've done some work for you already on the house. Get me on the payroll and I'll help out."

"Well," I said, "Frank did tell me to hire somebody if I thought I needed help."

"There ya go," Danny said.

Jerry stared at Danny, like how dare he ask for money to help Frank Sinatra.

"Hey," Danny said, "I'm Italian, but I need to make a living. *Capice?*"

"I getcha," Jerry said.

"I sure ain't getting' comped at the Sands," Danny added.

Jerry raised a hand, as if to wave away any further justification from Danny.

"Okay," I said, "you're on the payroll."

"Get me the names, addresses and phone numbers of any employee who were hired in . . . oh, say the last six months."

"Okay."

"You talk with the other Rat Packers—Lawford, Sammy, even Joey Bishop. See if any of them have received threats."

"I better talk to Frank first."

"Why?"

"I'll have to see if he objects to me talkin' to the others. It may be that only he and Dean know about Dean's threats. If I spill the beans to the others what if they take a hike? Get scared off?"

"Well, Sammy Davis doesn't strike me as the kind who scares," Danny said, 'but I don't know about the others. Okay, do what you gotta do, talk with Frank, first. And while you're at it, see if he'll let you talk to all the guys in the movie. Somebody might know somethin', and the only reason they're not talkin' is that nobody is askin'. It's my experience that unasked questions don't get answered."

"Got it," I said.

"You ain't gonna write none of this down?" Jerry asked.

"I've got it all up here," I said, tapping my temple.

"That's okay," the big man said. "I gotta write a lot of stuff down."

I didn't know if that was true, or if it was Jerry trying to act dumb, again.

"What's good ol' Jer gonna be doin'?" Danny asked.

"I'm gonna do my job," Jerry said, before I could say anything. "I'm gonna keep yer friend, here, alive."

"Suits me," Danny said.

"Suits the hell out of me, too," I said.

# Forty-two

WE PARTED COMPANY in front of the Horseshoe. Danny walked to his office while Jerry and I drove back to the Sands. This time I got behind the wheel of my own Caddy.

"That guy any good?" Jerry asked in the car.

"He's very good at what he does," I said.

Jerry nodded, but didn't comment.

As I drove down the strip, Jerry craned his neck to look at all the marquees. Nat King Cole was in town, along with Alan King and Shecky Greene. Buddy Hackett and Patrice Munsel were at the Riv. Donald O'Connor was playing the Sahara.

The one he paid special attention to, though, was the big Sands marquee that said Frank Sinatra, Dean Martin, Sammy Davis Jr., Peter Lawford and Joey Bishop.

"I don't get it," he said as I pulled the Caddy into the Sands lot.

"Get what?"

"The actor," he said, "Lawford. What's he doin' up there with the rest of those guys?"

"He's part of the group, isn't he?"

"I guess," Jerry said. "I don't get it, though. He ain't got no talent."

"He's an actor."

"So what's he doin' on stage with those guys?" he asked again. "I can even see Joey Bishop, he's a comedian, he kibbitzes with them. What's the actor do?"

"I guess you'll have to take in the show and see for yourself."

"Yeah, maybe."

As we entered the casino Jerry asked, "Whatta we gonna do now?"

"You can take some time off," I said. "I've got to talk to somebody in the employment department, get Danny that list of names he needs."

"You don't need me to watch your back?"

"I don't think I need my back watched while we're inside the Sands," I said.

"And whatta ya gonna do after you get the list?" he asked.

"That's when I'll have to talk with Frank."

"I can arrange that."

I was about to say no, and then I thought, why not? He was working for Frank and could probably get in to see him easily.

"Okay," I said. "Okay. See if you can set it up for later today."

"Consider it done."

"I'll have to talk to Dean, too. Then Sammy and Joey Bishop."

"Those guys I don't know so good."

"Don't worry," I said. "I'll set it up with Frank. I just need a few moments of his time tonight."

"You got it."

"I'll meet you in the lounge in two hours," I told him. "Can you get in to see him and be back by then?"

"No problem. He wants me to report to him each day, anyways."

"On me?" I asked.

"Not on you," he said, "just . . . about you. You know, whether you're okay or not. How you're holdin' up."

That was how Frank and Dean knew I'd been through something "intense."

"Yeah, okay," I said. "So I'll see you later."

"In the lounge," he said. "You need me before the two hours, that's probably where I'll be."

So just as we'd done with Danny a little while before, we split up and went our separate ways.


There was two ways I could go about what needed to be done. I could go to Jack Entratter and have him get me the list. Or I could go to the source itself. Marcia Clarkson worked in employment, kept the records of everyone who worked in the Sands. Without Marcia nobody at the Sands would get paid. Next to Jack Entratter, she was probably the most important person in the place. Hell, maybe she *was* the most important. I didn't know Jack's deal with Frank Costello, so maybe Marcia controlled his paycheck as well.

I went to the second floor, where the Sands' business offices were. I walked past Jack's office and headed down the hall to Marcia's inner sanctum. When I entered she looked up from her desk and smiled at me.

Marcia was pretty, there was no two ways about it. Her brown hair was kind of frizzy, and her glasses were so thick they magnified the beautiful blue of her eyes. She was in her mid-thirties and one might have called her mousy, but I knew her better than most. We'd gone out a few times. Nothing had developed romantically; now we were friends.

"Hello, Eddie," she said. "What can I do for you?"

"I need a big favor, Marcy." Yeah, I knew her well enough to call her by her nickname, the one family members usually used.

"Is this gonna get me in trouble?" she asked, raising one eyebrow.

"I don't think so."

"Is it something I'm gonna have to check with Mr. Entratter about?"

"Definitely not," I said. "I've got carte blanche from Jack. Access to anything I need."

"For what?"

"A favor I'm doing."

"For Mr. Entratter?"

I shook my head.

"For Frank Sinatra and Dean Martin."

Her eyes widened and for a moment I thought they'd leap right through her glasses at me.

"Is this on the level?"

"Cross my heart."

She looked around her small office, even though it was just her and me in the little room, and lowered her voice.

"Can you get me in to meet him?"

"Meet who?"

"Frank Sinatra, of course."

"Well . . ."

I almost felt bad now that I had taken Bev to see the Rat Pack show and not Marcia.

"We might be able to take in their show and then go back stage."

"Might?"

I nodded.

"First I have to do this favor for you?"

"Right."

"And I have to do it without asking any questions?"

"Right again."

"I'd feel better if you let me clear this with Mr. Entratter."

"Sweetie," I said, "I want you to feel better, so call him."

"Really?"

"Go ahead. I'll wait."

She picked up her phone, dialed three numbers, spoke to Jack's girl and then got put through to him. They talked for only about a minute and then she hung up.

"He says I'm to give you whatever you want."

"Why am I not surprised."

"And," she added, "he says for you to get your ass into his office the minute you're done here."

Still not surprised.

# Forty-three

"YOU WANT WHAT?"

I hadn't expected her reaction to be so violent.

A list of—"

"I know," she said, cutting me off. "A list of all of the employees hired by the Sands in the past six months."

"How many could there be?" I asked.

"Hundreds!" she said. "Do you have any idea how many people work in the casino and the hotel?"

"Oh." I hadn't thought of that. "Okay, try this. How about a list of the hotel employees?"

That calmed her slightly.

"Well . . . the hotel doesn't have as quick a turnover of personnel as the casino does. Mostly the dealers, you know? They come and go."

"I know." As a pit boss I saw them come and go.

"Not to mention the waitresses."

"So, can you do it?"

"Oh, it was never a question of can I do it," she said. "Just how long it will take."

"How long will it take?" I asked.

"A few days."

"I need it faster than that, Marcia."

"Boy, you don't ask for much, do you?"

"I also need you to have it ready for Danny Bardini to pick up."

"Bardini?" she asked. "That good-looking private eye friend of yours?"

"That's the one."

"Hmm," she said. "How about this? I'll work late tonight and have the list ready by morning."

"So far, so good. What's the catch?"

"That he takes me to see the Rat Pack show, and then we go back stage to meet Frank Sinatra."

"Deal," I said. Danny had never met Frank. He might enjoy that, and he might enjoy Marcia, too. They were two of my favorite people, why not put them together?

"Then get out of here and let me get to work."

I was almost out the door when she shouted, "Wait!"

"What?"

"Maids, too?"

"Oh, definitely," I said. "Maids, too."


"What the fuck?" Entratter said when I walked into his office. He looked as if he was about to explode—literally. It wasn't anger, really, more puzzlement, but his big shoulders and deep chest looked as if they were going to burst from his jacket, and his tie seemed to be strangling him. As if on cue he reached up to pull it away from his neck.

"Sorry?"

"Two girls are dead?"

"And one man," I added. "Mike Borraco."

"From the Riviera?"

"That's right."

"The fuck is goin' on, Eddie."

"I wish I knew."

"Why the hell are you gettin' involved in this when you have another job to do?"

"Well," I said, "I didn't know it when I found the first girl, Jack, but it seems to be all the same job."

"What?"

Briefly—quickly—I explained what was going on, and what had transpired out at the warehouse they were using for an *Ocean's 11* set.

"So you're tellin' me that you've found out that the threats against Dino are real?"

"With three people dead already, I would say so." I left out the part about Jerry shooting Buzz Ravisi, and Ravisi accidentally killing his own partner.

"And what do the police think?"

"Apparently," I said, "they're lookin' for Lou Terazzo."

"Unlucky Lou? They wanna pin this on him?"

"You don't think he could've done it, Jack?' I asked. "Out of jealousy, maybe."

"Jealous of Mikey Borraco?" Entratter made a rude noise.

"Jack," I said, carefully, "do you know something I don't know?"

"About what?"

"What the fuck, Jack—"

"You know, Eddie," he said, suddenly calm, "your Brooklyn comes and goes. Did you know that?"

"Yeah, Jack," I said, "I know that. Look, I've got to talk to everybody in the Rat Pack, and that includes hangers-on—"

"Hangers-on?"

"You know, Henry Silva, Richard Conte—"

"Don't let those guys hear you call them that," Entratter warned.

"Angie Dickinson," I went on. "But before I do that is there somethin' you wanna tell me?"

"No, Eddie," Entratter said. "I don't know what's goin' on anymore than you do. Go ahead and talk to everybody. Do your job."

"When did this become my job?" I asked. "And not a favor for a friend?"

Before he could answer the phone rang. He picked it up, listened for the second, then said, "What the fuck do they want? They're what? In my casino?"

He slammed the phone down.

"You know a guy named Jerry?"

"Yeah," I said. "Frank sent him to watch my back."

"Yeah well, Entratter said, "I guess somebody shoulda been watchin' his."

"What are you talkin' about?"

"The cops are in the casino right now," he said.

"What for?"

"Apparently," he said, "they're arrestin' him."

# Forty-four

WHEN I GOT DOWN to the casino floor in front of the lounge the police had Jerry Epstein in handcuffs. Two uniformed officers were flanking him, while Detectives Hargrove and Smith were fronting him.

When Hargrove saw me coming he turned my way and smiled.

"Just the man I wanted to see," he said. "We were comin' to look for you next."

"What's going on?" I demanded. "Why do you have this man handcuffed?"

"Well, Mr. Gianelli," Hargrove said, "he's under arrest."

"For what?"

"Suspicion of murder."

I looked at Jerry, who stared back at me with no expression. Just for a second I thought he gave me a head shake. Don't say anything, he was warning me.

"Who is he supposed to have murdered?"

"A coupla guys in a flophouse off the strip," Smith said. "Maybe you heard of them? Anthony 'Buzzy' Ravisi and Lenny Davis? They pretty much ran in your circle."

I looked at Smith for a moment and held my tongue, even though I knew what he meant. I didn't know how long he'd been a detective but there was a time when, even though he was a police officer, he would not have been permitted to make an arrest because he was a Negro. Things were changing, but not that much. I didn't know if he was looking down his nose at me and my Italian ancestry or if he was just an asshole.

"Forgive me, Detective, but you don't know what circle I run in. And I don't know what circles these men ran in."

"Pretty much the same as this joker here," Hargrove said. "You got imported New York muscle workin' for you, and you expect us to believe you don't run with the same company?"

"Jerry doesn't work for me, Detective," I said.

"Then what's he doin' here?"

I could feel Jerry's eyes on me, waiting to see if I was going to give Frank Sinatra up. I can't say I wouldn't have, if the cuffs had been on me, but I knew he'd cut out his tongue before he spoke Frank's name. Or Mo Mo Giancana's, for that matter.

"He's gambling, as far as I know. Spent some time playing horses yesterday."

"That's not all he did, yesterday."

Hargrove turned and put his hand out. One of the uniforms handed him Jerry's .45, holding it by the trigger guard.

"He killed two people with this gun."

Well, I knew that wasn't true. Jerry had killed one man with that gun.

"Once I prove it, he'll be up for murder, and you," he said, "will probably be locked up as an accessory."

"Accessory?"

"That's what we call people who are present when someone is murdered," he explained, "and who help the murderer."

"Detective," I said, "I really think you've got the wrong guys—"

"We'll see," he replied, "once our witness gets a look at the two of you."

"Are you takin' me in?" I asked.

"Not yet," Hargrove said. "First we'll have him ID Big Jerry, here. Once that's done, we'll have you in for a lineup. Meanwhile, don't even think about leavin' town. That would sort of be the same as a confession, don't you think?"

"I'm not goin' anywhere, Detective," I assured him, with much more confidence than I was feeling at the moment. "I'm not guilty of anything." There you go, I thought, a bold-faced lie.

"We'll see about that." he turned to the two cops holding onto Jerry. "Take him out."

"Jerry," I said, "the Sands will get a lawyer for you."

"I'm not worried," Jerry said to me. "I'll be out before the end of the day."

"I seriously doubt that," Hargrove said. "Get him out of here."

"Detective," a voice behind me said.

I turned and saw Jack Entratter standing there. He'd straightened his suit and combed his hair, and he looked calm and collected. Still looked like he was going to burst out of his clothes, though.

"Mr. Entratter."

"Can we talk? Privately?"

"Sure."

I don't know what surprised me more, that they knew each other, or that Hargrove was so willing to talk to Jack.

He took the Detective into the lounge, up to the bar where they could both sit on stools. I turned and looked at Jerry. The two cops had started to hustle him away, but now they were waiting for further instructions.

"What are you waiting for?" Detective Smith demanded. "Get him out of here!"

Both of the cops were white and they simply stared at Smith and didn't move. They were obviously going to take their cue from Hargrove.

Smith turned and glared at me. He seemed angry that I had witnessed the lack of respect he commanded from the white cops. Not my problem, I thought, and looked away.

The conversation between Entratter and Hargrove was fairly animated, went on for a few minutes, and did not turn out the way I expected. I figured with Jack being all calm and charming he'd get his way, even if he had to pull out Frank Costello's name to do it. However, when they came back Jack was not looking happy.

"Let's go," Hargrove said to the cops.

"Uh, are we takin' him in?" one of them asked.

"Of course we're taking him in," Hargrove said. He turned to Entratter. "Have your lawyer ask for me."

"I'll do that, Detective."

Hargrove gave me a look, then turned and followed the other cops out. Jerry went along as meek as a kitten.

"He's fucked," I said to Jack. "When they run that gun he's screwed, and so am I."

"I don't think so."

"Why not?"

Entratter looked at me.

"That's not the same gun."

"What?" I asked. "How do you know?"

He smiled and said, "Because he got rid of it. I got him one just like it."

# *Forty-five*

I WANTED TO GO the police station to help Jerry get released. Entratter vetoed the idea.

"What can you do that our lawyers can't?" he asked. "Besides, if they decide they want to lock you up too, let them come lookin' for you."

"So what do I do?"

"What you've been doin'," he said. "What you planned to do. Let me worry about gettin' Jerry out."

I have to admit, part of me was wondering who would watch my back while Jerry was in custody. It was selfish, I know, but I'd already been around more violence in the past few days than all of my life—including a couple of years on the streets in Brooklyn.

The other part of me just wanted to get Jerry out. After all, I knew he'd killed Buzzy Ravisi in self-defense, and had saved my life in the process. I already owed him a lot.

"I'm goin' back to my office," he said. "What was all that about with Marcia?"

"Just a few things I needed," I assured him. "Nothing to worry about."

Jack pointed a big index finger at me.

"That's good," he said, "because I have enough to worry about.

Fix this Dean Martin thing, Eddie. I'm countin' on you, and so is Frank."

"I won't let you down."

Another bold-faced lie? That remained to be seen.


I got to a phone and called Danny Bardini. I told him he could pick the list up from Marcia in the morning and, oh yeah, he had a date with her.

"This the Marcia you went out with a few times?" he asked. "Frizzy hair, sexy mouth, whole eyeglasses thing goin' on?"

"That's the one," I said. "She's kinda special, Danny."

"I'm hip," he said.

"Then you'll do it?" I asked.

"I'll answer that after you tell me what it is I have to do."

"Easy," I said. "Just escort her to a Rat Pack show and then take her back stage to meet Sinatra."

There was a moment of silence, and then Danny said, "That means I get to meet Frank, too?"

"Yes."

"And Dean Martin?"

"Yes."

"And Angie Dickinson?"

"I don't know," I said. "If she's there . . . maybe." I still hadn't gotten to meet Angie Dickinson, myself. "I'll arrange for you to get back stage. Will you do it?"

"It's a sacrifice," he said, "but somebody has to do it."

With that done I told him how Jerry had been arrested.

"If he goes down he'll take you with him, ol' buddy," he warned.

"I don't think so, Danny," I said, "but I'm not all that sure he'll go down. Apparently, he's already dumped the gun, so their ballistics test is not gonna come up with a match. Our only problem is the witness."

"What witness?"

"That's the problem," I said. "I don't know."

"Eddie, if there's a witness that can ID you and him . . ."

"I know," I said. "It won't even matter that it was self-defense. They'll wonder why we didn't report it in the first place."

"Wait until they get a sheet on Jerry," he added. "I'll bet he's been a bad boy in New York."

"Entratter's gonna get him an attorney."

"Probably a mob attorney," Danny said. "That'll seal the deal."

"I guess we'll have to wait and see."

"Might as well get on with what you have to do while you're waitin'," he suggested.

"I know," I said. "Jack already told me that. I'll talk to you tomorrow."

"You gonna be there when I pick up the list?"

"Of course," I said. "I have to introduce you to Marcia."

"Was this date her idea, or yours?"

"Why would a date with you be my idea?" I asked.

After we hung up I wondered if Jerry'd had time to arrange for me to see Frank. The only way I was going to find that out was to find Joey Bishop, or have Entratter call down to the steam room for me.

Or, I could just go down to the steam room myself and see if I'd made the A-list all on my own.

# Forty-six

**W**HEN I GOT DOWN TO THE steam room I was surprised to see that all of the bathrobes were missing from the pegs. Apparently, every one of the Rat Packers were having a steam after the day's shooting. There were plain bathrobes in a closet. I debated for a moment whether or not I should go in, then decided, what the hell? It was as good a time as any to be properly introduced to the ones I hadn't met yet, and it was a good test to see how welcome I'd be.

I got undressed, donned a robe and entered the steam room.

"Whoa!" Sammy Davis said. "Who's the strange cat?"

"Take it easy, Smokey," Frank said. "This is Eddie G. He's a pit boss in the casino, and a new friend. Come on in, pally. Have a seat and I'll introduce you."

It occurred to me that this could get awkward. Sammy, Peter Lawford and Joey Bishop didn't know about the threats against Dino. Also, Peter and Sammy didn't know that Joey had brought me to Frank. So the only one who knew everything that was going on were me, Frank and Dean.

Frank made the introductions around the room, as if I didn't know anyone, except when he got to Dean he added, "And, of course, you know Dino."

"Yes," I said, "of course."

"I say," Peter said to me, "I think I saw you on the set today."

"That's right, Charlie," Frank said. "I gave the okay for Eddie to come and watch some of the shoot."

"Welcome to the club, Clyde," Sammy said. "Take in a steam with the cool cats."

"Thanks."

"Eddie," Frank said, "Sammy just asked me to be his best man. He's asked May Britt to marry him."

I looked at Sammy, who today was wearing his eye patch. I assumed the glass eye, which he wore on stage and in the movie, was not behind it.

"Really? That's great. Congratulations."

"Thanks, man," Sammy said. "I know there's gonna be some cats out there who are gonna get all bent out of shape, but we love each other. I don't care how many threats I get, I'm gonna marry 'er."

"Threats?" I looked at Frank.

"The usual things," Frank said. "that is, usual for Sammy."

" 'Die nigger,' " Sammy said, " 'die Jew.' I'm used to it, but it upsets May."

"Fuck 'em," I said. "Bunch of ignorant bastards."

"Hey, Frank," Sammy said, "I like this boy."

"Hey, Eddie," Dean said, "I might feel like dealin' some blackjack tonight. You gonna be in the pit?"

"I'm actually off the clock at the moment, Dean," I said, "but I can make a point to be in the house tonight."

If I had to stay in to let Dean do some dealing, it kept me from going outside without my backup man, Jerry. Given how close I'd come to physical harm, and even death, I didn't relish hitting the streets without him.

"Well," Dean said, stepping down off the risers, "I'm gonna hit my room and take a shower, get ready for the show." He slapped me on the shoulder. "See ya later, pally."

"I've had enough, too," Joey Bishop said. "See you fellas at the show."

"Yes, I suppose it's that time," Peter Lawford said. "I have to call Pat, anyway. Good to meet you, Eddie."

He waved as he went out the door. That left me with Frank and Sammy. I looked at Frank, to take my cue from him, but he and Sammy started talking about the wedding and I thought I should leave. Frank stopped me.

"You just got here, Clyde," he said. "Stick around. Sammy's gotta go anyway."

"May's waitin' for me," Sammy said. "See you later, Frank. Good to meet you, Eddie." He shook my hand, a fierce grip for a man so small in stature, but huge in talent.

"What a bunch, huh?" Frank asked.

"Yeah," I said, "it's good to have friends."

"You got friends, Eddie?" he asked. "I mean, a lot of friends?"

"Not a lot," I said. "A few good ones."

"Hang onto them," he said. "You never know who your true friends are. Some of 'em, they just need you, or wanna use you."

I didn't know what to say to that, so I said, "Frank, I need to talk to Sammy and Peter about threats."

"You just talked to Sammy."

"I mean, about the same kind of threats Dean's been gettin'."

"Why do you have to do that?" he asked, with a frown.

"What if one of them has been gettin' the same threats, but hasn't said somethin' about it?" I asked.

"Why would they do that?"

"I don't know," I said, "I'm just tryin' to come up with a next step. If one of them has been gettin' threats then we'll know they're not just bein' aimed at Dean."

He thought that over for a moment, then said, "I see your point. You'll have to talk to Joey, too."

"That's right."

Frank scratched his cheek and thought a moment.

"Try to do it discreetly," he said. "Don't tell 'em about Dean if you don't have to."

"What can I—"

"Just say your askin' all of 'em about it," he suggested, "even Dean."

"And what do I tell them is the reason?" I asked. "I mean, I'm just a pit boss."

"Tell 'em you're doin' it for the Sands. Tell 'em Jack Entratter wants to make sure they're safe in his hotel."

We both knew what they'd think, that Frank Costello wants to make sure they're safe. It would make them pretty sure I worked for Costello and, consequently *La Cosa Nostra*. I didn't like havin' anybody think I was mobbed up, but when it came to these guys, when was I ever going to see them again after they finished filming the movie? We just didn't travel in the same circles.

"Okay," I said, "I'll be discreet."

"Good. I knew I could count on you. So, how's Jerry workin' out for ya?"

"He got arrested tonight."

"What? When? Where? And for what?"

I explained that the cops had come to the casino and arrested Jerry on suspicion of murder.

"Did Jerry murder someone?"

"Well, no," I said, "He, uh, did kill someone, but it wasn't murder."

Frank looked disgusted.

"Why don't you tell me what happened, Eddie?"

"How much has Jerry told you?"

"That doesn't matter," he said. "Come on, give."

So I told him everything that had gone on, before and after Jerry. He listened intently and did not interrupt me once. I wondered how much of my story matched Jerry's, and why there would be any discrepancy.

When I was done he said, "Jesus, you've been through a lot."

"We—"

"And all to do me and Dean a favor?" he asked. "You sure Jack didn't threaten you and make you help?"

"No," I said.

"Maybe you should bow out," Frank said. "Stay healthy."

"Frank, I started this, I'd like to finish it."

"You sure everything is tied together?"

"The warehouse you're using as a set is where Mike Borraco was killed. Up to that point I thought everything was separate, but now I have my doubts."

"And you don't want to quit?"

"No, I don't."

"You're a stand-up guy, Eddie."

I didn't reply.

"Stay inside tonight," he said. "Dean says he wants to deal some blackjack, so you don't have to go out. Tomorrow you'll have Jerry back. Jack Entratter will see to that."

"Frank, I was just wonderin'."

"Wonderin' what?"

"Couldn't you ask some of your . . . friends for help?"

"Sometimes," Frank said, "askin' the wrong people for help is a sign of weakness, Eddie."

I guess that was supposed to answer my question.

"I've got to get ready for the show," he said. "You gonna be there tonight with your girl?"

"I don't think so," I said, "and Bev was just a friend, not my girl."

"Oh. When she turned down Nick Conte I thought she was your girl."

"No."

We left the steam room together. He dropped his robe and started to get dressed, so I did the same. I told him I had some friends coming to the show tomorrow night, and wanted to get them back stage. He said he'd arrange it. I gave him Danny and Marcia's names.

"The doll," he said. "Another friend?"

"Yeah," I said, "another friend."

He wagged his index finer at me and said, "Sounds to me like you got more than just a few."

"Maybe."

"Let's go, kid," he said, slapping me on the shoulder. "We both got things to do."

We made our way to the casino floor and stopped there.

"Listen, if things start to get really hairy, I can probably get you some more help," he said. "You just let me know."

"Okay, Frank. Thanks."

He nodded and went off to get ready for the show. Me, I stood there wondering how much hairier things could get.

# *Forty-seven*

I DECIDED TO TRY dropping in on Peter Lawford first. I had the feeling if I waited until the next day, Lawford wouldn't remember me. He struck me as being a very self-involved type.

I called up from downstairs and he told me to come on up, assuring me that I would not be bothering him. When I knocked on the door of his suite he called "Come in."

I entered and I saw he was on the phone. He waved at me to approach and pointed to a sofa. I noticed that his suite was not as spacious as Dean Martin's.

"Yes, Pat," he said into the phone. He was dressed casually in tan slacks and an open-neck white polo shirt. "Yes, dear." He rolled his eyes at me and I shrugged. His hair was wet, presumably from his shower from the steam room. I'd also had a shower, using the facilities the hotel made available to employees.

"Well, just tell Jack that Frank—" He stopped short and frowned. "I am not Frank's lackey, or his errand boy, dear." He was remarkably calm for a man whose wife had just called him those names. "Frank is devoted to helping Jack get elected. All I'm trying to do is my part for the family. Yes, well, you ask Jack if he wants Frank's help or not and see what he says. And then ask Bobby, see what he says." He listened again, then jumped in, as if he was interrupting her. "I have to go now, love. I have to get dressed for the show. Yes, I know I'm an actor, not a performer. I act like I'm performing."

Apparently, Peter's wife agreed with both Jerry and me about his presence on stage with great entertainers like the rest of the Rat Pack. I had never met the woman, but found myself liking her.

"Yes, I will," he said, leaning over to hang up the phone. "Yes . . . yes . . . yes . . ."

With the phone still against his ear he stooped down closer and closer toward the base, as if he was going to hang up any second.

"I love you too, dear," he said, and finally hung up. "My wife," he said, unnecessarily. "Are you married?"

"No," I said. "Never have been."

"Smart man. Can I get you as drink? Or a cigarette?"

"No, I'm okay," I said.

"I'm going to have one of both."

He walked to the bar, moved around behind it.

"I won't take up too much of your time," I said. "I know you have to get ready for the, uh, show."

"Yes," he said, pouring himself what looked like scotch. "Frank absolutely insists that I go on stage with he and Dean and the others. It's ludicrous, really, but there you are. One must keep the leader happy."

It sounded to me like he was talking about someone like Hitler, not Frank Sinatra.

The actor came around the bar with a drink in one hand and a cigarette in the other.

"What did you want to talk to me about . . . Eddie, isn't it?"

"That's right," I said. "Eddie. Mr. Lawford—"

"Oh, call me Peter, please," he said interrupting me. "Any friend of Frank's is a friend of mine."

"Uh, on the phone a minute ago," I asked, "the Jack you were talkin' about, that was JFK, right?"

"Our next president," he said, proudly, "if Frank and I have anything to say about it. Will you be voting for Jack Kennedy, Eddie?"

"I really don't know, Peter," I said. "The election is a long way off."

"Indeed it is, but we're working hard now too—oh, never mind that. You didn't come up here to talk politics, did you?"

"Now, I didn't," I said. "The Sands is concerned that you be satisfied with your stay."

"Is that why you're here?" he asked, surprised. "To see if I'm happy with my room?"

"Not exactly," I said. I went with a story I'd come up with just after leaving Frank. "Apparently some guests have been getting' threats. We wondered if you'd received any."

"What kind of threats?"

"Phone calls, letters, notes—"

"Death threats?" He looked concerned, took a good, long sip of his drink.

"Threats of bodily harm," I said. "We haven't really heard anything about death threats, uh, yet."

"You know, my wife is part of the Kennedy family," he said.

"I know that. Have you gotten any threats, Peter? Of any kind?"

"No, no," he said, "no, none . . . yet. Other guests have, you say?"

"Yes."

"Uh, regular guests, or celebrities?"

"I'm not really sure—"

"Because if someone is threatening the regular guests, well then, I suppose I'd have nothing to worry about, but if they're targeting famous people—this could get into the papers, couldn't it?"

"It might," I said. "Publicity is good for an actor, isn't it?"

"Normally, yes."

"Normally?"

"Well, with the election and all, Joe—uh, Jack's father, Joseph Kennedy is running JFK's campaign—Joe wouldn't like any bad publicity."

I wondered if Joe Kennedy considered mugging on stage with the Rat Pack bad publicity.

"So, you haven't been threatened?" I needed to get a straight answer from him.

"No," he said. "No threats."

"All right, then." I put my hands on my knees and pushed myself up. "I won't bother you with this anymore."

"If I do get threats, uh," he said, walking me to the door, "What should I do?"

I almost told him to call me, but in the end I simply said, "Call security. They'll take care of it immediately."

As I left I was thinking it sounded to me like Peter Lawford wouldn't have minded some bad publicity—or publicity of any kind, for that matter.

# Forty-eight

I HADN'T EXPECTED to see May Britt in Sammy's room with him, but I was doubly surprised to see May's mother was there, as well.

"Come on in, man," Sammy said. He'd answered the door himself, wearing a white shirt and black pants. "May and her mother were leaving to do some shopping." He pronounced her name "My." "Honey, this is Eddie—I don't know your last name."

"Gianelli," I said. "It's nice to meet you, Miss Britt. Congratulations on your upcoming wedding.

May Britt was a breathtaking beauty, with the blondest hair and clearest, smoothest skin I'd ever seen. I knew half a dozen casinos who would have hired her to be a showgirl on the spot, but she already had a career of her own as an actress. I wondered how much heartache was in the couple's future because of the differences in their race. As for her mother, it was easy to see where she got her looks from. Mrs. Wilkins was an older, slightly faded version of her daughter.

"Thank you very much," May said. I found her Swedish accent charming, and understood immediately why Sammy fell in love with her. "I'm very happy to meet you."

"Come, Mama," she said. "We must allow the men to talk."

"I'll see you later, baby," Sammy said, and they shared an affectionate kiss.

When the women were gone Sammy said, "Isn't she something?"

"She sure is," I said. "Beautiful. You're a lucky man."

"Wonder what she's doin' with a one-eyed black Jew?" he asked. I searched his face for any sign of belligerance, but there was none.

"No, Sammy, I don't," I said. "I imagine she sees in you what women are supposed to see in the men they love."

Sammy Davis Jr. laughed, slapped my arm and said, "You're all right, man. Drink?"

"No, thanks. You go ahead."

"Naw," he said. "I've got to get ready for the show. You wanted to ask me something?"

I found Sammy different when he wasn't around the others. He was more relaxed and comfortable with himself. When he was around Frank he seemed too eager to want to please him. I wondered why a phenomenal talent like him had to kowtow to anybody, even a Frank Sinatra. But I was also sure that there were things about Sammy's life, and his relationship with the other members of the group I didn't know, and would never understand.

However, I wondered if Sammy was not a member of Frank's "Clan," if he would have been allowed to stay in a suite at the Sands. Negroes were not allowed to stay in the casino hotels, then, not even entertainers. Jack Entratter, by giving into Frank's demand that Sammy be given a suite, was inadvertently leading the way to change things in Vegas, when it came to segregation.

I fed Sammy the same story I'd given Peter Lawford and he just shrugged.

"Hey, man, the only threats I been getting are the usual ones. Nothing new to me."

"Then I won't take up anymore of your time."

Sammy walked me to the door.

"Any chance I can get you to tell me what's really goin' down?"

"What do you mean?" He'd caught me off guard, but I thought I handled it well. Sammy Davis Jr. was no dummy.

"I mean you're a real cool cat, Eddie," he said. "Why would Jack Entratter waste your talents on an errand like this?"

"Sammy, I—"

"Forget it," he said, quickly, waving my response away. "Forget I even asked. When Frank or Dean want me to know what's goin' on, I guess they'll tell me."

He opened the door and I felt I had to say something to him while we were alone.

"Sammy, I just want to tell you that I think you're an incredible talent, and you seem like a nice guy." I heard myself gushing and tried to stop, but I was impressed with the man.

"I am a nice guy, Clyde," he said, with a smile.

"Well, I just want to say I wish you and May all the best, and I hope you won't let what some ignorant bastards say and think—ah, what the hell. I guess I don't know what I'm talkin' about, really."

"Yeah, ya do," he said. He took my hand in his powerful grip. "You know what you're sayin' just fine, Eddie. Thanks."

He released my hand and I stepped out into the hall. He closed the door gently, still smiling. I felt we connected in that moment, really connected. I thought how lucky I'd be if I could call Sammy Davis Jr. my friend.

# *Forty-nine*

HENRY SILVA and Richard Conte were not given suites in the Sands, but they were put up in good-sized guest rooms. I spoke to both of them briefly, giving the same story. Neither had received any threats. They also didn't seem to know that Dean Martin had been threatened. They thought Frank wanted them to accompany Dean to the set for another reason—to keep him out of trouble.

"Frank says Dean's havin' trouble with Jeannie, and might do somethin' foolish," Henry Silva told me.

Nick Conte had been told the same story by Frank, but I could tell he didn't believe it. Conte and Dean were close, coming from similar Italian backgrounds. But apparently Conte was like Sammy, willing to go along until he was told differently.

I wasn't able to find Angie Dickinson to speak with her. I was starting to think she was avoiding me.

I decided not to ask any of the others the same questions. I had a consensus now, and it seemed that the only one receiving threats was Dean.

For want of something better to do I decided to stick around the casino and wait for the show in the Copa to be over. Dean Martin had said he wanted to deal some blackjack tonight. He usually did that when there was a good-looking woman at the table. She'd bust with twenty-two and he'd change the rules and tell her she won. It also drew a crowd, which I wasn't convinced was a good idea tonight. I wished Jerry was around.

If I was going to be around the pit I'd have to dress better, though, but I wasn't about to go back home without Jerry watching my back. I decided to change into a suit I kept at the casino in case of an emergency.

I had showered and was standing in front of a locker, tying my tie, when Jack Entratter walked in. A couple of dealers I knew were also getting dressed in front of their lockers and looked nervous as Entratter entered. As far as I knew Jack had never been in that locker room.

"You boys finished?" he asked them. "Yer shift is about to start."

"Yes, sir," one of them said. They both got the message and hurriedly left.

"What brings you down here, Jack?"

"I've been lookin' for you everywhere."

"I was talkin' with Sammy and Peter Lawford, and a few of the others."

"You didn't tell them what's goin' on, did ya?" he demanded.

"I'm not stupid, Jack."

"No," he said, "sorry."

"But Sammy's no dummy, and Nick Conte knows Dean well enough to figure out something's up."

"Well, just leave it to Frank to fill them in when he's ready."

"That was my plan." I finished with my tie and slammed the locker door closed. I didn't lock it because I kept nothing of value inside.

"Why were you lookin' for me, Jack?"

"You goin' to the show tonight?"

"I wasn't plannin' to."

"What are you dressed for, then?"

I told him about Dean wanting to deal, and my promise to be around.

"I want you to go to the show. Here."

He reached in his jacket pocket, came out with a ticket and handed it to me.

"You need another one? Wanna bring a broad?"

"No," I said. "One's enough." I pocketed it. "Why do you want me to go?"

"Because I trust you, Eddie," he said.

"To do what?"

"The right thing."

Entratter had a lot of men at his disposal, most of them like Jerry—pros.

"What's this about, Jack?"

"I need someone to watch things, somebody who won't embarrass me and the casino."

"Embarrass you how? Come on, what's goin' on?"

He hesitated, then said, "You know about Frank supporting JFK for president, right?"

"Sure, who doesn't?"

"Well, he's gonna be here."

"Who's gonna be here?"

"Come on, Eddie, keep up," he said, irritably. "Jack Kennedy. He's gonna be at the show tonight."

"Wait . . . the man who might be the next president of the United States is here?"

"Yeah."

"Well, what am I supposed to do about it?"

"Just be there," he said, "and watch."

"Is his wife with him?"

"No," Entratter said. "So you can see the potential for trouble here? A handsome Senator, presidential candidate, in Vegas with the little woman at home?"

"I see your point."

"Where they go tonight," Jack said, "you go. Promise me, Eddie."

"What about Dean? He wants to deal."

"If Frank takes Kennedy out, Dean will either go along, or just go to his room. So let him deal, and then see what he wants to do. If he's in his room he'll be okay. If he goes along, you'll have to go anyway, to watch him."

"I'm no bodyguard, Jack," I said. "What about Jerry? Is he gonna get out tonight?"

"I don't know," he said. "We're still workin' on that. You gotta help me out, Eddie."

"This goes above and beyond work, Jack," I said. "Or even our original, uh, favor."

"I know, I know," Entratter said. "I'll owe you, owe you big-time."

It wouldn't hurt to have Jack Entratter indebted to me.

"Whataya say?" he asked, anxiously.

"Yeah," I said, "okay, why not? A night out on the town with Sinatra and JFK? Where's the harm in that, right?"

"No harm at all," he said, and then added, "I hope."

# Fifty

THERE WAS A HUM in the audience. JFK was sitting in the mezzanine and everyone was aware of his presence. They had to be because of his bodyguards. They stuck out with their broad shoulders and their scowls.

Kennedy himself was all smiles as he sat with a few men, but no women. As much of a womanizer as the world and I would come to know him to be in coming years, he was discreet in public, back then.

At one point Frank stopped the show to introduce "the next President of the United States, John F. Kennedy."

I had a front row seat on this night, and from what I could see it looked as if Dean wasn't as thrilled with JFK's presence as Frank was. At one point Dean approached the mike and asked Frank, "What did you say his name was again?"

Frank gave Dean a look, but laughed. I wondered if and when politics would come between these two good friends?

The jokes flew after that, all at Kennedy's expense, and he seemed to love it. When JFK was elected Sammy was to become Ambassador to Israel. Frank would be Ambassador to Italy. Joey Bishop had a much less grandiose request—he just didn't want to be drafted ever again.

The show was a huge success, as always, but on that night the applause in the room was as much for John F. Kennedy as it was for the Rat Pack. Being Frank Sinatra's friend was putting Kennedy over with the Everyman big time.

As it turned out, Dean didn't deal blackjack that night. Frank had everybody up to his suite, including Kennedy. The champagne and booze flowed, and Sammy came in at one point with a bunch of showgirls in tow. Kennedy was in his element, smiling, back-slapping men and flirting with beautiful women.

At one point I saw Sinatra introducing Kennedy to Judith Campbell, a stunning brunette. I remembered how the other night Campbell was not too thrilled to have Bev back stage. She seemed very territorial when it came to Frank. Now Frank was pushing her toward Kennedy, who was only too happy to catch her.

"Look at 'im," Dean Martin said, coming up alongside me.

"Frank, you mean?"

"He's gonna help get Kennedy elected, you know," Dean said. "And then he's gonna find out the truth."

"What truth?"

Dean looked at me.

"There's no room in an Irish Catholic White House for wops, Eddie," he said. "Frank thinks he'll be a guest at the White House after the election."

"And he won't?"

"Not a chance," Dean said. "Joe Kennedy will see to that. And you know what else? He's gonna blame poor Peter."

"When did Frank become so interested in politics?" I asked.

"He's been a dedicated Democrat since he met FDR years ago. He was very impressed that a kid from Hoboken could actually end up shaking hands with the President."

I studied Dean to see if he'd been drinking, but he looked stone sober.

"Look, Eddie," he said, "I can see where this party's goin'."

He pointed to a showgirl who was taking one of the men with

Kennedy into a bedroom. I wasn't sure if he was a politician or a bodyguard, but it was a safe bet he was going to get the blowjob of his life tonight. I looked around and saw another pairing being discussed in a dark corner.

"This could go on all night," he said. "I'm gonna go to my room and catch a Roy Rogers movie on late TV."

"I'll come with you—"

"No, no," he said, "you stay here, have fun. I'll be fine. I'm not going to leave the hotel."

"What about Frank?"

"You tell him where I went," Dean said. "I'll see you all tomorrow. We're gonna be shooting at the Riviera and the Sahara."

"Dean—"

He slapped my back and said, "Have fun, pally. Grab one of those cuties for yourself."

I watched him walk to the door and let himself out. His suite was just down the hall, so I knew he'd be fine. Besides, Entratter had wanted me to watch Sinatra and Kennedy. I looked around, saw Frank, Kennedy and Judith deep in conversation. Kennedy had his arm around her waist, and she had her breasts pressed against him.

Dean was right. It was going to be a long night.


Everything became sort of a blur after that. More booze, even more showgirls, and at one point I found myself in a corner with Peter Lawford and Sammy Davis Jr.

"You fellas want to see what a million dollars in cash looks like?" Peter asked.

"You gonna pull it out of your pocket, Pete?" Sammy asked.

"It's in a leather satchel in the closet of one of the bedrooms," Peter said. "The hotel owners got together and are donating it to Jack's campaign."

I lost track of both of them and never knew if they'd gone in to look at the money. I didn't. I'd been behind the cages and in the counting rooms of the Sands. I'd seen a million dollars in cash and more before.

✳   ✳   ✳

I felt something warm and smooth press against me and turned into it. Using my hands I discovered that it was a naked ass, and a very nice one, at that. Firm and round, just the way I like 'em.

I opened my eyes and looked around. My own bedroom, and my own bed. The girl had clear, smooth, pale skin and a mass of black hair. That was all I could see. I didn't remember getting there, and I sure didn't remember bringing a dame with me. I wondered which of the showgirls had managed to snag me.

I hate forgetting women's names, but in this case I just couldn't dredge it up. I had a hangover, so I knew that I had started drinking after Dean left the party. The headache wasn't that bad, though, and I did have a warm and presumably willing woman in bed with me. Between us my dick had started crawling up the crack in her butt and there's wasn't much I could do but go with it.

"Ooh, baby," she said, reaching behind her to take hold of me. "What a nice way to wake up."

"Roll over," I said into her ear, "and I'll show you a nicer way."

"Mmm, an invitation I can't refuse."

She rolled onto her back and the first thing I saw were her breasts, big and firm, with dark brown nipples. Okay, so I'm a pig. I looked at her face second, and was stunned.

"What are you waiting for, lover?" Judith Campbell asked me with a dazzling smile.

## Fifty-one

FIRST CAME THE SEX, because I'm only human. I wasn't about to kick a naked Judy Campbell out of my bed. We went at it like teenagers and I thoroughly enjoyed her and didn't wonder until later if I had slept with Frank Sinatra's girl, John F. Kennedy's girl, or—according to some rumors I'd heard—Sam Giancana's girl. When a broad is naked in your bed, nothing else matters at that moment.

"You really don't remember?" she asked later, over coffee.

"I'm sorry," I said, "but a lot of last night is missing."

"That's not something a girl likes to hear, Eddie."

"Hey," I said, "I was thoroughly conscious this morning."

"Yes," she said, "I did notice an improvement in your performance over last night."

"That's not somethin' a guy likes to hear, Judy," I complained.

She laughed and said, "Forget it. I'm, just kiddin' you. We were both so tired and drunk last night that we went right to bed—to sleep."

"Okay," I said, "but what I'm wonderin' is . . . how did you come to be with me?"

"If I remember correctly," she said, "you invited me home."

"Yeah, but . . . you were with Frank and Kennedy."

"Frank doesn't care who I fuck," she said, "as long as he gets to fuck me when he wants."

"And Kennedy?"

"Well, there were some sparks," she said, "but nothing's happened yet. It will, though."

"And us?"

"Us?" She laughed again, but this time I had the feeling it was at me. "Eddie, this was just for fun. One night. No strings."

"Oh," I said, "suits me."

She reached across the table and put her hand on mine. She was wearing a white shirt she'd taken from my closet. I've always thought a woman wearin' a man's shirt like that is sexy as hell. Judith Campbell wearin' a man's shirt like that was even sexier.

"You don't seem as happy to hear that as most men would."

"Well, face it, Judy," I said. "You're gorgeous. What man wouldn't want you?"

"A lot of men want me," she said, "just not for very long."

"Why is that, do you think?"

She shrugged.

"I'm a party girl, Eddie," she said. "I'm not ready to settle down with one man, so it doesn't concern me."

"You sure know who you are and exactly what you want," I said. "I've got to admire that."

She reached out with both hands now, grabbing mine, and said, "Right now I want you to do more than admire me."

I squeezed her hands and asked, "What happened to just one night?"

"This is morning," she said, "an extension of the night before. Don't tell me you don't want to lay me one more time? For old time's sake?"

My answer was to drag her into the bedroom.


I called a cab for Judith and she went back to the Sands, to a room Frank had arranged for her. I'd been with a lot of women before Judith Campbell, but never with anyone quite like her. I hoped she'd get what she wanted when the time came.

Once she was gone I showered, got dressed and had some more coffee. Then I made a few phone calls. Penny told me Danny had already gone to the Sands to pick up the list. She didn't mention his date to take Marcia to the Rat Pack show that night, so I didn't either.

Next, I called Jack Entratter.

"Where are you?" he demanded.

"Home. I just woke up a while ago."

"Well, you did good last night, kid," he said. "I heard Kennedy never left the hotel, and I haven't heard about any trouble on his floor. I guess you kept the lid on for me."

"I guess I did, Jack. What about Jerry?"

"He's out," Jack said, "back here at the Sands. His gun didn't match. They were pretty much able to tell that right away. They kept at him all night, though, and he gave them nothin'. Never mentioned your name, or any anyone else."

"A stand-up guy." Frank had said that about me, but it applied more to Jerry.

"Any cops lookin' for me?" I asked.

"Not here," he said. "I don't know about anywhere else."

"Okay," I said. "I'll be around in a while. Tell Jerry not to go anywhere without me."

"He won't leave until you get here. I upgraded him to a suite. Kind of like a reward."

"Good," I said. "He deserves it."

I hung up, couldn't think of anymore calls to make. Frank and Dean were probably still asleep in their rooms. If everything I'd heard about Frank was true, he had two broads with him.

I decided to go for breakfast, then head for the Sands. My car was out front, so I must have driven it home. As I turned the key to start the engine I realized I'd forgotten my wallet. I got out, left the car running, and started for the house. A moment later I felt something lift me into the air and toss me across the lawn. I didn't hear the blast until later. . . .

# *Fifty-two*

THAT SHOULD HAVE BEEN IT for me.

Okay, I got beat up. Okay, if not for Jerry I might have gotten shot by Buzz Ravisi in that flophouse. But now somebody had tried to blow me up. Someone had seriously tried to kill me. That had never happened to me before and it wasn't the kind of new experience I was interested in having.

Pieces of my car were lying all around me, some of them burning, while the remainder of the car was ablaze at the curb. When I turned and looked at my house I could see that the front windows had been blown out. Some of my neighbors—the ones I didn't hate and who didn't hate me—came running out to see what happened, then came over to see if I was all right. The ones who did hate me came out to bitch about the noise or about their windows. They were talking to me but I couldn't hear a thing except a kind of dull hum in my head. Finally, someone called an ambulance, which arrived in tandem with a Sheriff's Department car. They put me in the ambulance and took me to the nearest hospital. I think I blacked out once on the way, because when I woke again I was in the emergency room. Still couldn't hear, so the doctors and nurses asking me questions were an annoyance. I just kept shaking my head and shrugging. They finally gave up trying to find out where it hurt—or whatever the hell they'd been ask-ing me—and gave me a complete once-over.

Yeah, that should have been it for me. Why go on when some-body obviously wanted me dead this bad? And for what? For what?

Well . . . I didn't know, and maybe that's why it wasn't it for me. My curiosity wouldn't let it rest. What did I know, or what was I do-ing, that made somebody want me out of the way this bad? This . . . well, permanently?

So, that should have been it for me, but it wasn't. The first thing I should have done when my hearing came back—if it came back—was march right up to Jack Entratter, Frank Sinatra and Dean Martin and say, "Sorry guys, I'm out."

But I wasn't going to do that.

You know why? It was more than just my curiosity.

For the first time since I'd started this whole thing I wasn't afraid, or puzzled or confused.

Now I was mad.

# Fifty-three

BY THE TIME they put me in a hospital bed, my hearing had started to return. However, when Detectives Hargrove and Smith entered the room I had a miraculous relapse.

"Can you hear me, Mr. Gianelli?" Hargrove asked.

I heard him, but it sounded as if he was standing at one end of a tunnel, and I was at the other. But I just stared at him and shook my head.

"Your doctor tells us your hearing loss is temporary," he went on.

That was good to know, but I didn't let on that I'd understood him.

"I think he's fakin'," Smith said, glaring at me.

"The guy got blown up, Willie," Hargrove said. "Somebody put a freakin' bomb in his car. The doctor said he's deaf."

"Temporary," Smith said, "the doctor said it was temporary. What if he already has his hearing back and he's scammin' us?"

Hargrove looked at me. I tried to stare back at him with a look of total innocence on my face.

"You wouldn't do that to us, Eddie, would you?" he asked.

"I'm sorry guys," I said, and shrugged.

At that moment the doctor walked in.

"Come on, doc," Detective Smith said. "Can he hear or can't he?"

"We'll know when he tells us," the doctor said. "Right now I need for you gents to leave."

"Okay," Hargrove said, "but we'll be back. After all, we have to find out who tried to kill him."

"I'm sure he'll be glad to help you with that when he can," the doctor said.

The two detectives left, Smith tossing me one last hard stare. The doctor approached the bed and looked at me curiously. He was in his forties, with steel-gray hair and eyes and a strong jaw. I was sure he made all the nurse's knees weak when he walked the halls.

"You'll have to talk to them eventually, you know," he told me.

"I will," I said. "How did you know?"

"Experience," he said. "Let me take a look at you."

He used a light to check my ears and eyes.

"You have a concussion," he said. "We're gonna keep you here all day and overnight just to be on the safe side."

"Fine with me," I said. "Can I have visitors?"

"Who'd you have in mind?"

"I don't know," I said. "Frank Sinatra?"

He laughed.

"If Frank Sinatra walks into this hospital I'll let him visit you," he said, going along with what he thought was a joke.

"Fair enough," I said.

"My name is Montgomery," he said. "If you need anything that a nurse can't give you ask for me. I'll be on until six. I'll look in on you before I leave."

"Thanks, Doc. And thanks for not tellin' the cops I can hear."

"Well, I wasn't really sure, was I?" he asked. "I assume you'll be ready to cooperate with them tomorrow? I mean, you do want to find out who did this to you, don't you?"

"Oh yeah," said. "I just need some time to think."

"I don't believe I'd need time to think if someone had put a bomb in my car," he said, "but it's your call."

I looked at the phone on the table next to me.

"Can I use that?"

"Why not?" he asked. "You're going to be paying for it."

As he left the room I leaned over, picked up the phone and set it on my chest. I dialed Danny's number, and when Penny answered I didn't tell her what happened. I just asked for Danny. When he came on I gave him the news.

"What the hell," he said. "Are you okay?"

"I was deaf for a while, but it's comin' back to me," I explained. "I scammed the cops, though, into thinkin' I was still deaf."

"Why?"

"I'm not sure," I said. "I guess I'll have to think about that."

"Well, I'll come over and help you think," he said. "You want anything?"

"Just don't bring any flowers."

After I hung up on him I dialed the Sands and asked for Jack Entratter. When I told him what had happened, he exploded.

"What the fuck is goin' on?" he demanded. "Somebody put a fuckin' bomb in your car?"

"Looks that way."

"You stay put," he said, "and do what the doctors tell ya. Don't worry about nothin'. The bills'll be paid for."

"Thanks, Jack."

"I'll be there in a little while," he said. "I got some calls to make. You're done with this, Eddie. You hear me? You're done."

"No, Jack, wait—" I started, but he hung up.

Physically, I felt pretty good. I had a few aches and pains, but nothing was broken. And I knew a concussion wasn't life threatening. I'd known enough football players who'd gotten five or six during their careers. And boxers. One wasn't going to kill me.

My hearing was getting better by the minute, which was a relief. I probably could have gotten out of that bed and walked out of the hospital, but I didn't want to—not just yet. I needed someplace quiet and safe to think, and this was as good a place as any. If I wasn't going to back off, then I needed to plan my next move.

# *Fifty-four*

THE NURSES WERE VERY ATTENTIVE, but when I told them I didn't need anything they left me alone. That gave me some time alone before Danny or Jack Entratter arrived. When Danny did get there I'd thought it out pretty well. Now all I needed to do was talk it through with someone and have them point out all the mistakes I was making. Danny Bardini was perfect for that.

"Well, well," he said, when he walked in, "I thought I'd find you all bandaged up from head to toe."

"I was pretty lucky."

"I know," he said, shaking my hand and then holding onto it. "I talked with your doctor. Apparently the blast picked you up and tossed you a good distance. It also threw you clear of flying debris."

"See any cops on your way up?"

"As a matter of fact, I did," he said. "There are still some sheriff's deputies around, and I saw your buddies, Hargrove and Smith. Apparently, the sheriff's office has handed your case over to them completely, given their previous experiences with you."

"I guess that's okay," I said. "Maybe they'll actually figure out who did this. Can I have my hand back now?"

Abruptly, as if he didn't know he'd been holding it, he let it go. He grabbed a chair, pulled it over to the bed and sat down.

"You were lucky, Eddie," he said, seriously. "Whoever wired the car knew what they were doing. Hargrove can't explain it, but there was a hesitation when you turned the car key and the blast didn't go off right away. What happened? Why weren't you in the car?"

"I realized I forgot my wallet," I said. "I was walkin' back to the house when it went off."

"Jesus," he said, shaking his head. "You gonna give this up now and hand it over to the police? Rat Pack and all?"

"I had a woman with me last night, Danny." I didn't tell him it was Judith Campbell. "I called her a cab this morning. If I'd offered to drive her home she would've been in the car."

"More good luck," he said.

"Well, bad for somebody," I said, "because now I'm pissed off."

"Eddie . . ." he said.

"What?"

"You're a long way from the streets of Brooklyn," he said. "You got out of there, went to college, became a CPA and somehow ended up in the pit at the Sands."

"Your point being?"

"You may work for some hard guys, my friend," he told me, "but you ain't a hard guy. Let the cops handle it, or let the boys handle it."

"I wish I could, Danny," I said, "but this ain't right. Too many people have died already, and for what?"

"I don't know."

"And I don't know," I said, "but I wanna find out. This must have to do with something other than some threats against Dean Martin."

"Did you ask them all about threats?"

"I asked," I said. "Dean's the only one."

"The threats, them dead girls, Mike Borraco, and now this," Danny said, shaking his head.

"You get that list from Marcia?" I asked.

"I got it, but it's gonna take a while to go through all those people."

"Too long," I said. "We've got to come up with something else."

"Like what?"

"I don't know," I said. "I wish Jerry and I coulda found out who hired Ravisi and Davis."

"Wishin' ain't gonna do you any good, bud," Danny said.

"I know."

"Why don't you spend a quiet night here and think about it in the mornin'," he suggested. "You want me to come and pick you up?"

"No, I'll have someone from the Sands do it. They're gonna cover my bill."

"Okay, then." He stood up, reached out to touch my arm, then stopped. "Take it easy."

"Don't forget you have a date tonight," I said. "Enjoy the show."

"I will," he said, then added with an evil grin, "and I'm gonna enjoy your girl."

"She's not my—" I started, but stopped because he was already out of the room.


I didn't know I had fallen asleep until I woke up to find Jack Entratter standing by the bed.

"Hey, Jack."

"Eddie," he said. "How you feelin'?"

"Got a headache," I said. "Doc said I had a concussion."

"I thought they weren't supposed to let you fall asleep with that?" he said.

"I dunno," I said, hoarsely. "Guess I'll have to ask the doc. Is there any water here?"

"Water?" He picked up a pitcher from the table next to the bed. "Yeah, here's some." He poured it into a cup and handed it to me.

"Thanks." I drained it and handed it back.

"When you gettin' out?" he asked.

"Tomorrow mornin'."

"You wanna go home from here?"

"I dunno," I said. "Guess I'll decide that in the morning."

"I'll have somebody from the Sands come and pick you up."

"I appreciate that, Jack."

"No problem, Eddie," he said. "You're here because I made you talk to Frank. I feel bad about it."

"Don't, Jack," I said. "I coulda pulled out any time. I didn't."

"But you are now, right? I'll talk to Frank, and Dean—"

"No," I said. "I want to see this through."

"Eddie . . . whatayawanna get killed?"

"No," I said, "but I don't want to run, either. I want to do what I said I was gonna do, help find out who's threatenin' Dean."

"Frank and Dean ain't gonna think any less of you if you quit," he assured me. "Not after this."

"Jack," I said, "I think it's too late to pull out, don't you? I mean, somebody obviously wants me dead. They might come for me, anyway."

"You got a point," he said. "I hate to say this . . . never thought I would . . . but maybe you should go to the cops."

"I still have to think about it."

"Can't get rid of that tough Brooklyn guy inside you, huh, kid?"

"I was never that tough, Jack," I said. "Just kinda stubborn."

"I'm gonna get you all the help you need, Eddie," he said.

"You bring in some muscle, Jack, and we may never find out who was behind this."

"Why would that be so bad?" he asked. "Let's just scare 'em off."

"No," I said, "I want to know who put a bomb in my car." I wanted to know who had almost killed Judy Campbell, too. If she had been in my car I would have had to live with that all my life.

"Okay," Jack said, "okay, we'll play it your way. I'll still have you picked up in the morning."

"No argument."

"If you come to the Sands make sure you stop by and see me first."

"Yes, sir."

"I already spoke with the hospital," he said. "Don't worry about the bill."

"Thanks, Jack."

"Yeah, sure."

I thought I blinked, but my eyes must have been closed longer than that because when I opened them Jack Entratter was gone.

# Fifty-five

WHEN I OPENED MY EYES again I saw that I had another visitor. I also saw that it was dark out, probably well past visitor's hours.

"How'd you get them to let you in here?" I asked Jerry.

He turned from the window and walked over to the bed. I had recognized his broad back.

"I tol' 'em to try and make me leave," he said. "Nobody had the balls to do it."

"What are you doin' here, Jerry?"

"My job," he said. "Keepin' you safe."

"I'm in the hospital, Jerry."

"They can get to you here just as easy as out there, Eddie," he said. "Believe me, I know. I've seen it."

"You gonna stay awake all night?" I asked.

"That's the plan."

I stared at him. Was he doing this because Frank had told him to keep me healthy, or had we managed to bond over the past two days?

I really didn't care.

"Thanks, Jerry."

"Sure," he said.

"What happened with you and the cops—"

"Just go to sleep," he said, cutting me off. "I'll be here when you wake up. We'll talk about it then."

I wanted to tell him that was jake with me, but when I opened my mouth no words came out. . . .


Next time I opened my eyes the sun was streaming in the window. Jerry was still there, sitting in a chair, still awake.

" 'Mornin' " he said.

"You must be exhausted," I said.

"I had a few hours rest yesterday in a cell," he said. "It wasn't that bad."

"How'd the lawyer get you out?"

"There was no match with my gun, and the witness they had turned out to be not so good. He saw two men, one taller than the other, but no faces."

"So how did the cops know to come to the Sands to get you?" I asked. "And why talk to me about it?"

"You ain't so concussed," he said. "Them's good questions."

"Something' ain't right here," I said.

"With cops," he said, "nothin' is ever right. You ain't gonna get no help from cops on this, Eddie."

"I believe it."

"Yer gonna have ta count on me, and on yer friend Danny."

I knew I could count on Danny. But could I really count on Jerry? After all, he was Giancana's man on loan to Frank Sinatra. Seemed to me I was low man on the totem pole.

"First thing we've got to do is get me out of here," I said. "Jack Entratter said he'd be sendin' someone."

"That's me," he said. "I'll drive ya."

It was then it hit me that my beloved '52 Caddy was gone. There may have been a piece or two on my lawn somewhere, but it was gone.

"You thinkin' about your car?" he asked.

"Yeah."

"Yeah," he said. "That's a sin, blowin' up a car like that. Somebody needs to die just for that."

I agreed with him.


Jerry found my clothes in a nearby closet. I was dressed, sliding my feet into my shoes when a middle-aged nurse came through the door.

"Looks like you're cleared to leave, Mr. Gianelli," she said.

"Thank you."

She gave Jerry a hard look. I didn't bother asking what kind of run-in he must have had with the nursing staff the night before.

"Wait here while I get a wheelchair," she said.

"No," I said. "I can walk."

"A wheelchair is required, Mr. Gianelli," the nurse said. "Regulations."

"My man says he can walk," Jerry said to her. "He's gonna walk."

She glared at him again, seemed about to leave, then said to him, "You're a horrible bully!"

He looked at me with an expression that asked, What did I do to deserve that?

"She doesn't know what she's talkin' about," I said.

"Thanks. I just—"

"I think you're a helluva bully."

# Fifty-six

JERRY MADE ME WAIT just inside the front door while he brought the car around. Jack Entratter had given him a vehicle registered to the Sands, a black Mercury. As I got in and he drove off we were both silent. I knew we were each thinking about my late Caddy.

"Well," he said, breaking the quiet, "one good thing came out of this."

"What's that?"

"You ain't a suspect no more," he said. "Cops figure somebody tried to blow you up might be the same somebody killed those girls, and Mike Borraco."

"I guess that's one way of puttin' a positive spin on it."

"It ever happen to you before?"

"Never. You?"

"Once."

"What happened?"

"I got lucky," Jerry said. "Like you."

"Just a coupla lucky stiffs," I said.

"Better'n a coupla dead ones."

I couldn't argue with that.

\* \* \*

When we got to the Sands we both headed up to Jack Entratter's office, but Jerry stayed out in the waiting room while I went inside.

"You look woozy," he said.

"I'm fine."

"You shoulda went home."

"This is my home."

"Eddie—"

"I know what you meant, Jack," I said, cutting him off. "I don't wanna go home. I'm pissed, I wanna do something."

"Like what?"

"Kick some ass," I said, "I just have to find out whose ass to kick."

"Let it go."

"What?"

"Let the cops find who put the bomb in your car."

"We went through this last night, Jack," I said. "They're gonna keep comin' for me, whoever they are."

"I thought of that," he said. "I got an idea."

"What?"

"Get outta town."

"And go where?"

"Reno," Entratter said. "Frank's got a piece of the Cal-Neva. You can work there for a while."

"I appreciate the offer, Jack," I said, "but I can't do that."

"Eddie, if you get yerself killed, I'm the one's gonna be pissed."

"I appreciate the thought, Jack—"

"I'd have to replace you," he went on, "and good pit bosses are hard to find."

"I get it, Jack," I said.

"Keep Jerry with you."

"I plan to." I stood up. "What happened with the cops? I thought they'd be all over me when I woke up this mornin'."

"I got them to lay off ya," he said, "but they'll wanna talk to you later today. Not that you're a suspect no more—"

"Jerry told me."

"—but they figure whoever tried to kill you probably killed Borraco and those broads."

"They still like Lucky Lou for that?"

"Either that, or they just don't have any other suspects."

I sat there for a moment, going over it in my head.

"I can't see Lou tryin' to blow me up," I said, finally.

"Why?" Entratter asked. "Are you and him such good buds?"

"No, but—"

"If he did kill the two broads and Mike Borraco, he don't like you pokin' around, Eddie," he said. "You see Lou Terrazo comin' at you, I'd go the other way. Lou's a made guy."

"What?" I said. "I thought he was just . . ."

"Just what? Another mug? Naw, Lou made his bones in Chicago years ago. I gotta tell you, if you're on Lou's list . . ."

Christ, I thought, how stupid could I be? I worked in Vegas right in the midst of these guys. Just because I didn't think they were very bright didn't mean they weren't dangerous.

"What about Borraco?" I asked. Jerry had asked me if Borraco was made, but I didn't know.

"What, made? Mikey? Naw, not yet, maybe not ever. Mikey was a gopher, Eddie. If you had him pegged that way, you had him pegged right. But Lou . . . he's a killer."

So if Lou Terrazo was not only a killer but *the* killer, the cops were already on his tail. Did he think killin' me would get them off? Or was I just next on his list?

"So like I say, keep Jerry close to you."

"Oh yeah," I said, "close as a Siamese twin."

"A what twin?"

"Close, Jack," I said, "I'm gonna keep him real close."


I collected Jerry and we went back down to the casino floor. I realized that lately I had been prowling the floor without my customary black "pit-boss" suit, just going with slacks and polo shirts. I thought it was odd, so I wondered why nobody had been commenting on it.

But walking through the casino today I was getting comments about the bandage over my eye and the stiff way I was moving. Maybe people did care.

"I gotta go talk to Frank," Jerry said, suddenly. "He wanted to know when you got out of the hospital."

"Isn't he shooting at some of the casinos?"

"Yeah," he said, "tomorrow they shoot here. I think they're at the Riviera today."

"Well, go ahead," I said. "I'll be okay here."

"Don't leave or anythin' until I get back."

"I won't, believe me. I'm not goin' anywhere without you, Jerry."

That seemed to please him.

"I'll get back as soon as I can."

"I'll be around, down here on the floor, somewhere," I said, "or in the lounge."

"You want I should give you a gun—"

"Go!" I said.

"Okay, okay," he said. "I'm goin'."

He walked across the floor and out toward the front door. I turned and headed for the lounge. When I got there I saw that Bev was working, so I sat at one of her stations. Some baby-faced kid was on stage singing in what sounded like German. He didn't look old enough to even be in a casino.

"Are you all right?" she asked. "I heard what happened." Gently she touched my head near the bandage. "Why would someone do that to you?"

"Maybe it was a jealous husband," I kidded.

"Are you sleeping with other men's wives again, Eddie?" she scolded me.

"What do you mean, again?"

She laughed.

"What can I bring you. A beer?"

"No," I said. "Something that will numb the pain. Bourbon on the rocks should do it."

"Comin' up."

She turned and flounced off to the bar. I was watching her and didn't notice the man approaching my booth until he slid into it across from me.

"Don't make any sudden moves, Eddie," he said.

I looked at him and didn't recognize him right away. He was wearing a Dodger baseball cap pulled down over his eyes, which were covered by sunglasses. As a Yankee fan I found the hat offensive, but before I could say a word he reached across the table and grabbed my wrist.

"Hey!" I said. "What gives?"

"I got a gun pointed at you under the table," he said. "We're goin' for a walk."

"Who the hell—"

"What do you want to see first?" he asked. "My face or the gun?"

"Let's start with the face."

He released my wrist, lifted the ball cap and removed the glasses.

"Hiya, Eddie," Lucky Lou Terazzo said. "I hear you been lookin' for me."

# Fifty-seven

"JESUS, LOU," I said. "What the hell are ya doin'?"

"We're gonna get up and walk outta here together," Terazzo said.

I licked my lips and looked around. No one was looking our way.

"What if I don't wanna go?" I asked. "You gonna shoot me here, in front of all these people?"

"Why not?" he asked. "I killed three people already, ain't I? Three this week, that is."

Oh Christ, I thought, he just confessed to me. No way I was getting out of this alive. Why had I let Jerry go?

As if reading my mind Terazzo said, "I been waitin' for your big New York gun to take a walk. I ain't gonna miss this chance to take you out—not after missin' you last night."

"You blew up my car?"

He nodded.

"I did some demolition in Korea," he said. "Guess I was rusty, or you were lucky. One of the two. But now I'm gonna take you out myself, the easy way."

"B-but, why me? What'd I do to you?"

"You started askin' questions," he said. "I didn't need you askin' questions when I was plannin' on killin' Carla. I panicked."

"Why Carla?"

"She was cheatin' on me."

I didn't bother asking with who. That really didn't matter, in the long run.

"And why her roommate?"

"She got in the way," he said. "It was an accident."

"She didn't fall over the railing into the pool and drown."

"No," he said. "I hit her and she died. Simple as that. I dumped her into the filthy pool, figured nobody'd find her until I finished with Carla."

"And what about Mike Borraco?"

"He was helpin' you, wasn't he? Askin' about me? Come on, let's go."

"Wait." Even with my own death staring me in the face I figured this might be my only chance to find out if the killings were connected to the threats on Dino. "Why were you sending threats to Dean Martin?"

"What?" he asked. "Whataya talkin' about? What threats?"

"You weren't sending threatening notes to Dean Martin?"

"What the hell for?" He looked amazed. "I love the way that guy sings."

"But . . . why did you dump Mike's body at the warehouse they're using for *Ocean's Eleven*?"

"Hey," he said, "I was cruisin' Industrial Drive with a body in the trunk. I stopped at the first place I could find to dump it."

A coincidence?

"And what the hell did you come lookin' for me in the first place for?" he asked. "What'd I ever do to you?"

"I-I just wanted to ask you some questions about . . . about Dean Martin."

"Wait a minute," he said. "Somebody was sending him threats and you thought I'd know who it was?"

"I thought you might have heard rumors," I said. "I—I was stuck, didn't really know what to do next."

He glared at me, and I didn't know if he was going to laugh or cry.

"You just stumbled into my life? And ended up finding Misty's body?"

"That's the way it went."

"And you called the cops?"

"Lou . . . I'm sorry. I just—"

"Shut up!" he snapped. "Just shut up. Because you went bumblin' around I got to kill you, too. Let's go."

"Lou—"

"All I got to do is finish you and I can blow town."

"Blow town anyway, Lou. I won't say a word."

"Sorry, Eddie," Lou said. "You're a decent guy, but I can't afford to take the chance, ya know?"

"Yeah," I said, "yeah, I know."

"Here comes your waitress," Terazzo said. "She your girl?"

"She's got nothin' to do with anything, Lou."

"Well, you walk on out of here with me and she won't get hurt. *Capice?*"

"Yeah, Eddie, I *capice.*"

"Here's your drink, Eddie," Bev said, reaching the table.

"I just remembered I've got an appointment," I said to her.

"Don't I know you?" she asked Terazzo.

"Naw, you don't know me, girlie. Come on, Eddie."

Terazzo slid out of the booth. There was no gun in his hand, so I assumed it was in his belt.

"No, I think I recognize you—"

"No, you don't." I grabbed her hand, stuffed a twenty into it. "You don't know him."

We started for the door with Terazzo behind me when Bev called out, "Yeah, I remember. Lou Terazzo."

"Hold it!" Terazzo said.

"Forget it, Lou."

"Just stop. Turn around."

We both turned, and when we did I saw that Terazzo did have his gun in his belt, at the front of his pants.

"C'mere, sweetie," he said to Bev.

Suddenly, Beverly looked uncertain, as if she realized something was going on she didn't understand.

"I—I got to finish my shift—"

"Your shift is finished." He pulled his jacket back to show her his gun. "Now c'mon over here, or your boyfriend gets it."

"Lou, let 'er go—"

"She knows me, Eddie," Lou said. "I can't." He looked at Bev. "Now, sister. Move!"

Bev looked around the lounge, but everybody was listening to the fresh-faced kid on stage go into his next song. Nobody was paying any attention to us.

She sidled over to us and Terazzo made her stand next to me.

"Now we're all leavin', nice and quiet," he said. "Like three happy friends. Got it?"

"Eddie—" Bev said.

"Just do as he says, Bev," I told her, "It'll be all right."

We left the lounge and Lou said to me, "Take us out a back way, Eddie. Come on. You know this place inside and out."

I tried to think of a way to get Bev away from him, but he wouldn't give me the time.

"If we run into somebody in security, or anything like that," he told me, "I'm gonna start shootin'. You got that?"

"I got it."

I led the way, deciding to use what was the least-traveled path in the casino. I took him down the hall leading to the stairs that went down to the Rat Pack's steam room. Only instead of going down we continued on until we got to a back door. When I opened it and we stepped out we were in the parking lot behind the Sands. Terazzo looked around and, satisfied that we were alone, took out his gun.

"Right here, Lou?" I asked.

"It's as good a place as any. Plenty of cars for me to grab."

"You'd have to shoot us and then hot-wire one," I said. "Why not just take my keys?"

"Nice try, hot shot, but I blew your car up, remember?"

Shit!

"Wait," he said, looking at Bev. "Where's your car?"

"It's out here, but my keys are in my purse."

"Where's your purse?"

"In the lounge, behind the bar."

"Fuck!"

"Lou—"

"Shut up," he said. "I'm tryin' ta think."

Bev looked at me, biting her lower lip, and I winked with a lot more conviction than I felt.

"Okay, we'll hot-wire a car and then I'll take care of you two. Come on, I like that red one over there. Both of you, move."

"Red?" I asked, as he pushed us along. "That's kinda conspicuous, ain't it, Lou?"

"Don't matter," he said. "I'm headin' right outta town. Nobody's gonna be lookin' for me."

"What about your bosses?" I asked. "They're gonna be pissed when they find out what you did."

"Whatta they care? Besides, they ain't gonna find me, either. Stop."

We stopped by a red Corvette.

"You've got expensive taste, Lou."

"Look," he said, "it ain't even locked. I'll bet some high roller left his key in it. Take a look."

I peered into the car.

"No luck," I said. "You'll have to wire it."

"And I'll need both hands," he said. "Nice try. You do it."

"Me? I can't hot-wire a car."

"Didn't I heard you say one time you were from Brooklyn?"

"That doesn't mean I can steal a car."

"I can."

We both looked at Bev.

"What?" Terazzo asked.

"I can jack a car. I used to do it when I was in college."

Terazzo grinned.

"My kinda girl." He laughed. "Maybe I'll take you with me, honey. How would you like that?"

"I'll get the car started," she said, "but to tell you the truth I'd rather you shoot me with him then take me with you."

Terazzo lost his smile. Suddenly, he backhanded her across the face.

"Bitch! You're all bitches. Don't move, Eddie. Don't be a hero."

My muscles had tensed and I might have jumped him but he stuck the gun in my face.

"Open the door for the lady, Eddie," he said. "She'll get the car started, and then we'll decide who gets a bullet first, you or her."

I opened the door. Next thing I knew I heard Terazzo grunt. I turned and saw that a hand had come over his shoulder and grabbed his gun hand by the wrist. He was turned around abruptly and before he could react a fist crashed into his face. He went limp and as he slid to the ground the hand holding his wrist came away with the gun.

"I don't know what this is about, pally," Dean Martin said, "but I hate to see a lady get hit."

# Fifty-eight

I FINALLY GOT to drink my bourbon, only this time I made it a double. To Bev's credit she insisted on continuing her shift.

"If I go home I'll just sit in a corner and shake," she said. "But as scary as it was, at least I get to know that my life was saved by Dean Martin!"

That was looking on the bright side, all right.

Dean had come back from the Riviera after filming before the other guys. He spotted me with Bev and Lou Terazzo, started across the parking lot towards us, but increased his speed when he saw Lou smack Bev. He waited around long enough to hand the gun to a cop, then went to his suite, where he said he'd be available to make a statement. He told me to come up and see him when I was done.

True to his name, "Unlucky Lou" had picked the wrong day to come at me head-on, and was on his way to jail. I was nursing my bourbon, waiting for Detective Hargrove to come and question me for what I hoped was the last time. While I was sitting there Jerry came walking in.

"What's goin' on?" he asked. "I seen cops outside."

"Have a seat and a drink," I said, "I'll tell you all about it."

By the time I finished he was staring morosely into his beer.

"You coulda got killed," he said, "and it woulda been my fault."

"First of all," I said, "I'm not dead, and second of all, don't try to take all the credit. I let him walk right up to me."

"This was my job," he said. "I'm the pro, not you."

"Jerry," I argued, "you did your job, kept me alive in that fleabag and got hauled in for it." I picked up my glass and raised it to him. "Here's to pros."

He raised his glass, but still wasn't completely satisfied.

"I guess I better check out and head back to New York."

"Stay an extra day," I said. "I'll show you some of Vegas you didn't get to see."

"I s'pose I could stay one more night. I'll just have to tell Frank—"

"I'll arrange it with the hotel," I said. "And come to the show tonight."

"Frank said I should come whenever I wanted," he told me. "So, okay. I'll see the show. I heard they're hilarious together."

"They are."

He drained his beer and said he'd see me later. On the way out he passed Danny, and the two men sized each other up.

"What's goin' on?" Danny asked, sliding onto a stool next to me. "Cops outside, and big Jer looks like somebody took the bullets out of his gun."

"Have a drink," I said, and I told him about it just as I had Jerry.

"Jesus," he said, "Dean Martin saved your ass?"

"That he did," I said, "and I'm very happy about it."

"So the killer's off the streets."

"He confessed to me," I said. "I'll make a statement to Hargrove and that should be that. Now if I could just wrap up my original job . . ."

"I've got something for you on that."

"From the employee list?"

"No. I've had my ears to the ground and something came up to-day."

I put my drink down.

"Okay, give. If we could wrap both of these things up in one day I could go back to my pit, where nobody tries to kill me."

"Yeah, they just wish you dead."

"Danny . . ."

"I got somebody who saw your two dead goons, Ravisi and Davis, meet with a big man in a bar off the strip. Money changed hands."

"So they lied about bein' hired on the phone."

"Maybe," he said, "and maybe they were payin' off a gamblin' debt."

"You don't have a better description of the man they met with?"

"Big guy, expensive suit, wide shoulders. Could be Big Jer, except for the suit. His is more off-the-rack Robert Hall."

"No, not Jerry."

"Well, whoever he is, he's your insider."

"Then find me somebody on that list you got from Marcia who matches the description."

"Sure," he said, sarcastically, "that'll take no time at all."

"I'm gonna go up and talk to Dean."

"Take me with you."

"You'll meet him tonight. Besides, I gotta thank him for helpin' me out when I'm supposed to be helpin' him. It'll be a little embarrassin'."

"Hey, one more thing," he said, as we headed out. "My man says this big guy in the bar was always holdin' his head, you know? Like he was in pain all the time?"

We walked out of the lounge together then went our separate ways. I told him I'd see him at the show. His last comment to me had given me the answer I needed. Now I had to decide what to do with it.


Mack Gray opened the door to Dean's suite. He was still wearing a dark suit and white shirt, like the first day I met him. In fact, it could have been the very same suit. He also still had that pained expression on his face I'd come to know.

"The Boss is gettin' changed," he said, letting me in. "You wanna drink?"

I stared at him for a few seconds and he had to ask me again.

"Huh? Oh yeah, sure. Bourbon, rocks."

We walked to the bar together. He went around behind it and I sat on a stool. While he got my drink I went over it in my head and it fit. I was basing it on some pretty skimpy evidence, but there was only one way to find out for sure.

Ask.

# Fifty-nine

N OT HAVIN' ONE?" I asked when he pushed my drink over to me.

"No."

I sipped it.

"Let's cut to the chase, Mack," I said. "I figure you did it because you wanted Dean to need you a little more. Maybe he doesn't depend on you so much after eight years, or maybe just not as much as Mr. Raft did."

He didn't answer, didn't look at me, but I thought I saw his shoulders hunch.

"Or maybe," I said, "you're afraid he's gonna ship you off to someone else the way Raft did."

"The Boss didn't have a choice," Mack said. "He was broke. I told him I'd stay with him for nothin', but he said no. So I ended up workin' for Mr. Martin."

"And he became your boss."

"Yeah."

"But you're still loyal to Raft?"

He glared at me, now.

"I'm loyal to both of them," he said. "They're great guys."

I stared at Mack. He must've been about fifty-four then. Moving on would not have been a very good option for him. Starting over somewhere else.

"So you sent the notes."

His jaw tightened and for a moment I thought he'd either ignore me or slug me. Instead, he turned, poured himself some scotch, then pulled a pill bottle from his pocket and took two. Percodan.

"Somebody saw you with Ravisi and Davis, Mack," I said. "Big guy in a dark suit, always holdin' his head like it hurt. That's you."

He looked down at the vial of Percordan in his hand, as if it had betrayed him. I continued.

"It only occurred to me later that while Frank referred to the notes as death threats, they never really said anything about dying. Even in a note you couldn't bring yourself to threaten Dean in that way."

"I sent one," he said. "I thought that would do it, but he never mentioned it. Then I sent another. He still didn't mention it—to me. Pretty soon I found out he was talkin' to Mr. Sinatra, and then to you."

"So when I came into the picture you stopped sendin' the notes."

"They weren't doin' no good, so yeah, I stopped," he said. "I didn't mean ta threaten the shootin' schedule. I wasn't trying ta force the boss into hidin'. I was just . . . I don't know what I was doin'."

"And then you hired Ravisi and Davis to scare me off."

This time Mack looked away.

"I never meant you no harm, Eddie," he said. "That's all they were supposed to do, scare ya. They wasn't supposed to hurt ya."

"Well," I said, "they did that."

I decided not to tell Mack that he was responsible for the two hoods getting killed. I figured they were no loss to anybody, anyway.

He drank down half his drink while I sipped some more of mine.

"So I guess you're gonna turn me in now, huh? Tell the boss it was me?"

"What good would that do?"

"What?"

"He'd probably fire you."

"Naw—well, yeah . . . yeah, I guess he might."

"I don't want you to get fired, Mack."

He looked at me with surprise etched on his face.

"You ain't gonna tell him? Gee, thanks, Eddie."

"Maybe you should, at some point, but I'm not gonna. The important thing is that the threatening notes have stopped, right?"

"Definitely," he said. "No more notes."

"If you want Dino to depend more on you, find another way, okay?"

"Okay. You got it."

Suddenly, we heard Dino's footsteps coming down the hall.

"What are you gonna tell 'im?" Mack asked, lowering his voice.

"I'm gonna wing it," I said, quickly. "Just go along with me."

He nodded and we both turned and tried to look as innocent as newborn babes as Dino entered the room, shaking his right hand.

"It's been a few years since I hit somebody for real," he said to us. "Had to soak my hand for a while."

"You want ice, boss?" Mack asked.

"No, Mack, that's okay," Dean said. "I could use a drink, though."

"Comin' up, boss."

"Just one before the show," he said, approaching the bar. "So Eddie, what happened down there after I left."

"The guy you hit was Lou Terazzo," I said. "He killed his girlfriend and her roommate, both showgirls at the Riv. He also killed a guy named Mike Borraco, who worked with him there."

"Was it a sex thing?" Dean asked, accepting a glass of amber liquid from Mack. I hadn't watched him pour it, but I assumed it was bourbon.

"Yeah," I said, "sort of a triangle, and the roommate got caught in the fallout. But here's the weird part."

"Tell me," he said, still flexing the fingers of his right hand, "I like weird."

"Lou Terazzo was the guy sendin' you the threats."

"Why? What'd I ever do to him?"

"He fancied himself a ladies man, modeled himself after you, even thought he could," I lied. "When he realized he was none of those things, he snapped."

"Are you kiddin' me?" Dean looked delighted. "You mean I got him myself?"

"Guess you didn't need me after all, Dean," I said. "Fact is, you saved me."

"Hey, hey," Dean said, "don't sell yourself short, pally. You worked your ass off on this. I'm not gonna forget it." He turned to look at Mack. "Ain't that right, Killer?"

That was Mack's nickname from the days when he was a fight manager, before hooking up with George Raft.

"That's right, boss," Mack said. "His ass."

"So no more notes," Dean said. "That's good. And the guy's in the slammer."

"For a long time," I added.

"I'll have to tell Frank," Dean said. "He was worried, you know."

"Yeah, I know." I put my glass on the bar and got down from my stool. "Guess I'll be back on the clock now. If you want to deal any blackjack the rest of the time you're here, let me know."

I took it easy on his sore right hand as we shook.

"You really did save my bacon out there today, Dean," I said. "Not to mention Bev's. Thank you."

"We're even, Eddie," Dean said. "That's the way I see it."

"Okay."

He walked me to the door with his arm around me.

"You comin' to the show tonight? There's somebody I want you to meet."

"Milton Berle's comin' tonight," Mack said. "And Mr. Sinatra's new girl."

"New girl?" I asked.

"Yeah," Dean said, "we won't be seein' Judith around tonight. Juliet Prowse is coming. Gorgeous dancer. What a pair of gams!"

"Sounds like I shouldn't miss it," I replied. "I'll be there."

"Come back stage after and I'll introduce you around." He squeezed my shoulder when he said that, and then released me so I could go out the door. I found it an oddly touching gesture, like he was saying we were friends now.

# Epilogue

Y OU OKAY, Eddie?"

I opened my eyes and looked around. I was the center of attention, a circle of people standing around me, looking down at me with worried or curious looks on their faces.

"I'm fine," I said. "Where the hell am I?"

Sheldon Adelson said, "You passed out. We called an ambulance. You're lyin' on a gurney."

"Well, get me off," I demanded. "I'm fine."

Actually, I was better than fine. All that Rat Pack stuff had passed through my head while I was out—was it seconds? Minutes? Whatever it was I appreciated it. I would much rather have those memories of the Sands than any from the implosion tonight.

"Come on, somebody help me up!" I demanded.

Sheldon and Wayne Newton stepped forward and helped me sit up and get off the gurney. I looked at Wayne and could still see the fresh-faced kid in there who came to Vegas so many years ago. He patted me on the back affectionately and turned to leave. I knew he had his own memories of the Sands.

I looked at my watch. I'd been out about twenty minutes.

"You want me to take you home, Eddie?" Sheldon asked.

"I've got my car, Shelly," I said. "Don't worry about me. It was just . . . you know, the dust and . . . everything . . ."

"Yeah, I know, Eddie," Sheldon said, "I know."

The crowd was starting to disperse and I decided to get to my car and turn on the air-conditioning. I was still feeling kinda woozy, but I didn't want anyone to know.

I reached my Coupe Deville and got inside. I still liked Caddies. I started the engine, turned up the AC and put my head back. For one more moment I was back in the Copa Room at the Sands in 1960. Frank, Dino and the guys would leave Vegas on February 18th and head to Hollywood to finish shooting *Ocean's 11* there. The movie would be a big hit, and the guys would go on to make a few more—except for Peter Lawford. After Kennedy got elected he'd snubbed Frank and never let him come to the White House. Oddly enough, Frank never blamed JFK. He blamed Peter, and after 1962 the two never spoke again. I didn't like Peter much, but I thought he got a raw deal from Frank.

But that night in the Copa Room in 1960 the show went great. I saw Danny and Marcia enjoying it from their front seats, and I hoped the two would get along. But I didn't expect much, because Danny was a ladies' man and not ready to settle down. They had a ball, though, especially when they went backstage and met Frank and the guys.

While we were all backstage Dean came over to me and clapped me on the back again.

"Glad you made it, Eddie. Come on, I wanna introduce you to somebody."

I had already shaken hands with Milton Berle, and Frank had introduced me—briefly—to the beautiful Juliet Prowse, so I didn't know who Dean was taking me to meet.

But even now, thirty-six years later, I smiled in my Caddy as I remembered Dean Martin walking me up to a vision of loveliness, the owner of the best legs in Hollywood, and saying to me, "Eddie, I'd like you to meet Angie Dickinson."

*Author's Note*

THIS BOOK GREW out of my own respect for Dean Martin, Frank Sinatra and Sammy Davis Jr. as entertainers—not necessarily in that order. My posthumous thanks goes out to these three men for years of enjoyment through their films, their albums and their appearances on stage.

The books also comes from my love for the history, the pulse, the excitement that is Las Vegas. There's no other place in the world like it.

Believe it or not, research is an enjoyable thing. You just have to be careful not to get caught up and lost in it. The following books were hard to put down once I picked them up and instrumental—in large part or small—in making my book fun and interesting to write and, hopefully, to read. I acknowledge them, and their authors, here:

*Rat Pack Confidential* by Shawn Levy, Doubleday, 1998.
*The Rat Pack: The Hey-Hey Days of Frank and the Boys* by Lawrence
    J. Quirk and William Schoell, Taylor Publishing, 1998.
*Dino: Living High in the Dirty Business of Dreams* by Nick Tosches,
    Dell Publishing, 1992.
*His Way: The Unauthorized Biography of Frank Sinatra* by Kitty
    Kelley, Bantam Books, 1986.

*Gonna Do Great Things: The Life of Sammy Davis, Jr.,* by Gary Fishgall, Scribners, 2003.

*The Peter Lawford Story: Life with the Kennedys, Monroe and the Rat Pack* by Patricia Seaton Lawford, Carroll & Graf Publishers, 1988.

*Mouse in the Rat Pack: The Joey Bishop Story* by Michael Seth Starr, Taylor Trade Publishing, 2002.

*The Frank Sinatra Film Guide* by Daniel O'Brien, BT Batsford, 1998.

*The Last Good Time: Skinny D'Amato, the Notorious 500 Club, and the Rise and Fall of Atlantic City,* by Jonathan Van Meter, Crown Publishers, 2003.

*Casino: Love and Honor in Las Vegas* by Nicholas Pileggi, Simon & Schuster, 1995.

*Las Vegas Is My Beat* by Ralph Pearl, Bantam Books, 1973, 1974.

*Murder in Sin City: The Death of a Las Vegas Casino Boss* by Jeff German, Avon Books, 2001.

Of course, it was necessary for me to view the original film *Ocean's 11* several times, which was no hardship since it is a favorite of mine. My thanks go out to Warner Bros. and the cast and crew. The remake of several years ago was but a pale imitation. The original has taken a bad rap over the years. I think the guys did what they were supposed to do, the story held up, and I have always loved the irony of the ending.

My thanks also to Kathy War, photo archivist, UNLV Libraries, Special Collections Department, for the time and effort she put into talking with me and providing me with archive photos of the Sands Casino. As always my gratitude goes out to Marthayn Pelegrimas, for her love, support, and willingness to edit my manuscripts so they come out readable.